AS GRAY AS BLACK & WHITE

FAITH KNIGHT

ISBN 978-0-9826190-7-0

1

The day Billy demanded my Mickey Mantle, all the color drained from my face. My daddy gave me that card just before he died, and I swore I'd never lose it, come hell or high water.

Well, high water's done come, and Mama hurts like hell, so I slip it into my pocket and head to practice.

My stomach grumbles as I sit huddled together with the Crimson Sons on a wooden bench, close to the diamond. The guys who play with me put all they've got into the game. Last year, we did so well we almost made it to the state championship. We have to get there this year, and I want it so bad I can taste it.

"Here's the roster." Billy Justice, our team captain, stands before us, holding a wrinkled piece of paper that's the key to our future. His dirty blonde hair is mussed up and falls over his eyes. His cap is half-cocked, and his face is red and blotchy. Coach Collier allows him to deliver all the final decisions about the players.

Billy squints as he goes down the list of those who made the team and those who didn't. "On first, we're going with Ray, since that colored kid who tried out wasn't so hot..."

Sweat forms on my upper lip and my cheek's twitching. If Coach Collier doesn't pick Eddie to pitch, well, we just won't get to the championship, that's all. When Eddie came to tryouts, he brought a confidence to the pitching mound that none of the others dared. Not in front of an all-white team. He stood taller than most of us and what an arm! I swear that ball traveled 80 miles an hour on the first pitch. The guys called him 'Fast Eddie,' along with a few not-so-friendly words. His color didn't matter to me though. All I saw was talent. I pray Coach Collier did, too.

"Second base goes to Winston. We don't need no colored there..."

Why is Billy dragging this out? He knows what we're all waiting for, me most of all. As shortstop, I need a good pitcher who's going to throw to me when it counts, especially since we'll likely be up against the Bixal Bloodhounds. They've beat our team for the last two seasons, and stealing bases is their specialty. If Eddie joins up with us and Ray's on first, we'll be the team's triple threat.

My stomach lets out a loud growl. Hank nudges me as if I can simply tell my gut to keep quiet. I just smirk at him. Hank's our catcher and a darn good one. He'd be a good guy if he didn't spend so much time with a kid like Billy. But the one thing I can say about the Justices, they do a good business in town—most every kid I know has a mom or dad who works at one of their factories. They also give kids after-school jobs. If I play my cards right, I might get one, too.

"And for pitcher, we're gonna take..."

I cross my fingers. I'd cross my toes, but my sneakers are too tight. Billy stops and looks up. Something's wrong. He drops the hand that holds the piece of paper and stares at Coach Collier like he's got a problem. Coach Collier tells him to keep reading. Assistant Coach Justice—Billy's dad—just shakes his head. Billy scratches under his cap and continues in a low voice.

"...Eddie Goshay."

I leap to my feet along with my pal, Bosley, who also cares more about winning than color. We tear off our caps, jump around, and smack backsides. My big toe feels loose, and I'm almost certain there's a hole in my sneaker. Then I realize my joy might keep me from getting that job I need, so I tone it down.

Coach Collier comes off the bench and stands before us. He's a husky sort of guy with broad shoulders and a drive to win. He's a former minor leaguer and was the team's coach long before I got here. His once-dark hair lost its battle with the grey, so he keeps his ball cap pulled down to hide it. His big wide ears hold it there.

"I know some of you are glad we got Eddie. I am too. He's a hell of a pitcher." Coach Collier says this while he watches Coach Justice like he's expecting him to argue about it.

"But I'm warning y'all, be careful. Since we're going to have a colored on this team, we got an uphill battle with the fans—especially at away games. So you keep your senses and your feelings to yourself. Not everybody's gonna welcome Eddie on the opposing teams either, and most are gonna show it, but he's your teammate now, so treat him like one. Now get out there, and let's get to work. I'll give Eddie the news, and he'll join us tomorrow."

Billy's twisted face tells me he's disgusted. I know he didn't want Coach Collier to pick a colored boy, but once we get a few no-hitters, he'll change his mind. That's when I go over and pull Mantle out of my pocket. The card's a little bent, but Mickey still looks good. I hate like the Devil to part with it, but if I'm ever gonna fill this empty stomach, I gotta do it.

"What's *that*, Lawson?" Billy leans close, inspecting the card with one eye closed.

"It's yours. See? The first Mickey Mantle ever. The one I told you about."

I hand the baseball card to Billy, and he passes it to his best friend Ray. I try not to let him see me cringe, manhandling my Mantle like that. Ray whispers to Hank. The three of them are thick as thieves.

"I don't know, Lawson," Billy says, taking the card back from Ray. "Come on around to dinner Sunday, and we'll see what my Pop says."

After that, nothing else matters, not even eating. In fact, my stomach doesn't make another sound.

I'm invited to Billy's for dinner on Sunday. Perfect.

For the rest of practice, my mind's on how close I am to getting a job so Mama doesn't have to work as hard, sick as she is.

I shake the last thought from my head and force myself to think about the *other* good news: how easy it's gonna be to finally beat the Bixal Bloodhounds with Eddie Goshay on the mound.

I first met Eddie during tryouts at Huntingdon Field a couple weeks ago.

"Hi, I'm Mark Lawson, shortstop."

"I'm Eddie. Eddie Goshay. Um gonna be your next pitcher..."

With that introduction we hit it off. After a few practices with Eddie on the team, I walk home with him 'cause we live in the same general direction, and just like I thought, he's pretty OK.

I know it makes some people uncomfortable seeing us walking together, but with our uniforms on I figure they accept it since most recreation in town is integrated. No one who passes us ever says anything. They either stare or ignore us.

As for me, I look forward to our walks. Eddie tells me stories about the Negro Leagues and his idol, Mr. Festus.

"Taught me everything I know," Eddie says as we walk. "He played catch with me in the yard just about every day until I got real good—just me, him, and an old tennis ball. Yep, he was probably the best pitcher there ever was. A 90-miler if there ever was one, and that ain't no lie."

Eddie looks at me, and a smile grows across his face, which tells me it probably is a lie, but I'm OK with it since it sounds good.

Carter Hill is a long stretch of road that cuts right through my neighborhood and separates the races, sort of like a line in the sand. On one side sits Alabama State College, a colored school, along with small shotgun houses and a few modest homes. On the other side, neatly cut lawns and fancy flowerbeds surround houses as big as mansions. That side has fancy street names too, like Myrtlewood, Magnolia, and Boultier. That last one's my street. Eddie lives on West Fifth.

Even though our team is integrated, our schools aren't, so I attend Haley while Eddie goes to Frederick Douglass. There are one or two colored kids at a few white high schools, but they're just tokens forced on the city as a test. Mobile and Birmingham already teach coloreds and whites together, and despite what Governor Wallace does to keep Montgomery segregated, we all know it's coming.

I ask Eddie how he feels about integrating schools.

"We only want what's fair," Eddie says with his head down.

He stops and faces me. "And don't think we need saving either. We're getting a good education on our own. We learn a lot of stuff you don't—about colored doctors and scientists and other important things. What we really want is the same supplies...and funding."

I look at him. *What's he know about stuff like funding?* Then he tells me his mother is a teacher.

"All we need is a level playing field, and we'll be all right."

"Does that mean you don't want to go to school with...us?"

I'm not sure of my words, and I hope I don't get his dander up, but I never get to talk to coloreds, and I really want to know. I wait. We walk. He doesn't say anything, so we keep walking. Then I watch him pick up a rock and throw it so far I have to squint to see where it lands.

"You see that rock?"

I don't, but I nod anyway.

"That's about as close as I want to be to white folks."

He grows another one of those slow smiles, but this time I get the feeling he's not lying.

My head lowers. I decide not to ask him anything else. We stop at the curb and wait for the green light to turn red so we can cross. It's the corner where we go our separate ways.

"If you had a choice," he says all of a sudden. "Which traffic light color would you be?"

My eyebrows frown. Since I'm not sure what he's after, I play along.

"Green...I guess. Yeah, green, so I can go." I take a deep breath 'cause my answer is pretty good and pretty obvious. "What about you?"

The light turns red, and we cross. He doesn't answer me until we get to the other side.

"I'd be red."

"Red?" I say. "Why red?"

To me, it's a dumb answer. Red means stop, and who wants to be stopped? Then I think, red is the opposite of green; maybe that's why he said it. Or maybe, he's so used to being kept from doing things, red just comes natural.

"I'd be red because it shows folks I stand for something. People respect red. They see the red signal, and they stop. They see the red sign, so they stop for that, too. Y'ever seen somebody stop for yellow? They don't pay it no mind. But red, they got to respect red." Then he gives me a smirk.

"Bet you didn't know a Black man invented the traffic signal, did you?" I shake my head. "Garrett Morgan. We got brains too, you know..."

My respect for Eddie grew that day and keeps on growing each time we take the long walk down College Street to Carter Hill Road.

Of course, the fans at our games don't share my feelings about Eddie. Each time he's up to bat or heading toward the pitcher's mound, the rumbling begins. It always starts with one or two angry voices. A man jumps to his feet, swings his fist at Eddie, and vows to "lynch the little nigger."

Then one or two more join in with catcalls and angry threats.

"How'd you let that nigger strike out my son?"

"Get that black nigger off the field."

"We don't need no niggers playing with our kids."

All of us hear it. None of us do anything about it. Not even Coach Collier. If it gets real bad, Coach goes out to the mound, puts his hand on Eddie's shoulder, and talks to him. Then the game goes on. I figure it's some kind of pep talk, but none of us can hear what Coach says, and I never have the nerve to bring it up with Eddie.

So I sit with my chin in my hands, and just like everybody else on the bench, I act like it's normal. Once. Just once, I think I see Eddie crack out there, but I could be wrong. I can't see so good that far, but he's wiping something away from his eyes. Maybe it's just dust. It's a windy day; rusty signs swing on their hinges. The creaking and squeaking sounds like crying. Maybe they weep for Eddie. Maybe that's why Eddie won't let his mama come see him play. His dad comes sometimes. He sits in the colored section outside left field. Even though he's supposed to be allowed to sit with the white parents, they don't let him. Eddie says Mr. Goshay is his biggest fan, and if it wasn't for him, Eddie might not be playing on an integrated team.

After one of our practice games, I'm grabbing my bat and glove, ready to head for home, when Billy walks up from behind and whacks me across the back with his cap. "I seencha walking home with Eddie the other day," he says, rubbing sweat from his forehead, underneath his dirty blonde hair. "What you trying to do?"

I turn to look at him. My eyes narrow. His do, too.

"Don't act like you don't know what I'm talking about." He sits on the bench watching me pack up. "You're about to mess up a good thing."

"What do you mean?" I ask him. Billy knows I'm not breathing fire and brimstone against coloreds like he is. Though I don't aim to make Eddie my best friend, I don't hate him either.

"You know you can't work for my dad and hang around no coloreds. Not even Eddie, 'cept right here on the ball field. It ain't proper, and we Justices expect all our employees to act proper." He pulls his cap down over his brow. "So you best take my advice now and let that nigger alone. Ya hear?"

He whacks my shoulder with the back of his hand and takes off.

I sit for a while and think about what's going to happen when the schools really integrate. When colored kids turn up in all the same places where we turn up. Who's going to decide what's proper then?

I look up and see Billy and his crew walk toward left field. I figure they're headed for home if they don't find something else to get into. No telling with those three. Last year they spent many a night jumping students over at the colored college and taking whatever they could. They asked me to go once or twice, but I said no. Mama would kill me, and Pa didn't allow that kind of stuff. He used to say, "Only a coward sneaks up on you in the dark."

I also see Eddie in the cage next to the fence, throwing practice balls. I want to head over and wait so we can walk home together, but I need that job at Justice Manufacturing. So I head off in the other direction and cut down Fairview instead of College Street.

Trouble is, I forgot we made plans to go fishing down by the golf course Saturday morning. Even though I'm not supposed to, I've been doing more than just walking home with Eddie. We've been hanging out. We have a good time, too. He takes me to places he likes to go, like Pappy's Sweet Shoppe and Laundromat, or the barbershop where Mr. Leroy pays him to run errands. Once Mr. Leroy sent us to go pick up something called a pig ear plate from the local dive. Never heard of one before that day, and man did it stink, but Eddie says his mama loves them, like most folks in his neighborhood. Something about the juice is real important. Mr. Leroy said if Eddie spilled it, he could forget about the five-spot he promised him.

Of course, since we haven't walked home together the past few days, I never get a chance to tell him our fishing trip is off. I don't see him in class because we go to different schools, and at practice, there's no time to talk. I don't feel good about treating him like this, but I don't have a choice. If Billy sees me with Eddie again, I can kiss that job goodbye.

Funny thing about Eddie, he seems to sense things. That's the only explanation I can figure when he sits beside me on the bench next practice and whispers that he's got plans for Saturday:

"I'm going to a demonstration with my mother. Dr. King is supposed to be there. I can't miss that."

"What you gonna to be demonstrating?"

"Ending segregation, what else?" Eddie looks at me like I was born yesterday.

"But I thought all you wanted was equal stuff so you could stay separated?"

I see in Eddie's eyes that he hadn't thought about that, but still he has an answer. "Dr. King says we have to desegregate first, then we have a better chance at getting our own stuff."

"Hush up," says Hank, nudging me to keep my eyes on the field.

I can tell from Eddie's attitude he's not mad at me for avoiding him. After practice, I get it into my head to wait and walk home with him. The others have already left, so they won't see me. As usual, Eddie stays behind to work on his fastball.

"Got that job yet?" Eddie asks, like he's the cat that ate the canary.

I nudge him in a playful way. "I know you think I'm an idiot for kowtowing to Billy, but you have to understand—"

"You think I don't? Your daddy's dead, and your mama's struggling. If there's one thing I can understand, it's being poor. I knew what was going on. I'm not four, you know." He smiles again, and I smile back. "So did you get it?" He waits for an answer like he's really interested.

"Not yet, but I'm sure it's coming. I'm sure I'll be moving boxes in the warehouse or sweeping up. You know, just basic stuff."

"Does it pay good?"

"Don't know yet, but anything is better than what I had, which was nothing."

We laugh.

"Hey? You think we could still go fishing?" I ask. "Maybe *next* Saturday? Eddie is silent for a moment. He smirks at me. "I'm serious. If you don't have a march to go to, I mean."

"Well, I guess it'll be all right. Let's meet tomorrow night and look for a good place to catch night crawlers. We're gonna need those."

As I finish my walk home, I can't help thinkin' of Eddie's father and the work he does. It's a far cry from anything I'd want to do. He's a butcher, and the first time I saw him, he inspected me like a side of beef. He wore a Civil War cap with crossed swords and the lid flipped up. Seemed to me like an odd thing for a colored man to wear, but Eddie says he does it to remind white folks they lost the war.

It's not unusual for folks in his neighborhood to swing by the house with a deer carcass for his father to cut and clean. They just fling it on the back porch and drive off. To me, it's an awful way to make a living, but if that was the only job I could get, I'd sure take it. Maybe even keep some of the meat for Mama and me if the boss lets me. Thank goodness I won't have to do that kind of thing. I'm getting a good, respectable job, and when I do, I aim to keep it.

———

The next day when I waltz into the school cafeteria, it's buzzing. Girls in black and white oxfords cram the long, smooth tables, pushing up cat-eye glasses and trying to swing their legs over the bench without looking unladylike. The boys are nearby, praying some girl will bat a lash. So they play it cool, snapping their fingers to the rhythm of a Beach Boys tune. Somebody smuggled in contraband: a transistor that's got the kids tapping and humming along. Giggles, grunts, and groans make up the lunch line, and the ring of the cash register keeps time with the beat.

My daddy always said, "If you want to hide something in plain sight, put it in a brown paper bag."

When something's in a brown paper bag, nobody questions it. Whether it's wrapped around a liquor bottle or rolled down over wads of cash, people don't ask what's inside. They know it's meant to be hidden.

The brown paper bag I bring to school every day hides something, too: my pitiful excuse for a lunch. Nobody knows what puffs up my bag each day, and just like all other things in brown paper bags, they're not supposed to know.

I step over one of the bolted benches and take a seat, holding an apple while I wait for Bosley to show. Like Winston, he's in some of my classes. None of the other guys are, or else we wouldn't get any work done; all we'd talk about is baseball.

Boz was one of the first kids to click with me when I got here last year. And judging by my uncomfortable conversations with Eddie, it's clear I don't make friends so easy. Guess that's why I went out for sports. I can get out of my skin on the ball field, but off the field, well, I'm not that social.

Before I can say, 'Jack Benny,' here he comes. His pant legs drag the floor over his penny loafers. And that brown sweater's seen one too many spins in the wash, but he's aces, and him sitting with me keeps the other kids from thinking I'm a lunchroom loser.

Even though we eat together, Boz doesn't know the secret behind my brown paper bag. Guys don't talk out in the open about stuff like that, but from the way he treats me at lunch, I figure he's onto it.

"Hey, Mark." He scoots onto the bench and slides until he's opposite me.

"Hey, Boz, how's tricks?"

I can tell he just got his crew cut shaped up. We're the two BBs. Blue-eyed and blonde. I never saw a barber 'til we moved to Montgomery. Pa used to cut my hair to keep it out of my eyes. You can get hurt on a farm if you can't see what you're doing.

Bosley's eyes move from me to my apple. "Didn't you have that yesterday?"

"I did, but I got Becky into another marble-guessing contest, and I won. So after she handed over her bologna sandwich, I decided I'd save this for today."

Bosley grunts at my brown paper bag. "You're gonna need a lot more than an apple to keep up with them Bloodhounds."

"Aw... I'm just starting with this. I got other stuff in here."

He takes his Jell-O from the tray, puts it in front of me, and hands me a spoon.

"What's that for?"

"I—I don't really like Jell-O... so you can have it." He smiles and lowers his eyes to his tray. He's got mashed potatoes, corn, and meatloaf with that mystery sauce on top. It looks funny, but the kids say it's good.

I smirk, but I keep the Jell-O. It's red. My favorite.

Not two seconds before I slurp down a spoonful of the wiggly dessert, here she comes. Becky Gilmore—the girl that won't go away. She slaps her palms on the table between Boz and me.

"Double or nothing, whaddya say?"

I shake my head. "Why don't you just give up, Beck? You're a bad guesser, and I've already eaten your lunch three times this week."

She frowns. Becky's one of those over-anxious girls who likes athletes and will do anything to nab one. She could be a real looker if she got rid of that white lipstick and all that black stuff on her lids. Reminds me of Cleopatra. 'Course it don't matter to me; I don't have time for a girlfriend. I got other priorities. Important ones.

"Mark Lawson, you're a pig-headed idiot." She folds her arms. "You're gonna be sorry you got me mad." She stomps off, her stringy ponytail swinging left to right.

Bosley raises his eyes to meet mine. "Girls." He finishes his tray, and I throw my apple core in my bag.

When he's gone, I take my bag to the trashcan. I make sure no one sees me as I turn it upside down and dump all the balled-up newspaper pages. I usually keep them, but that juicy apple core got 'em kind of wet. I fold the bag nice and neat and stuff it into my pocket.

———

When I get home from practice, I pull the mail from the box in front of our house on Boultier Drive. Our box is simple: white metal on a wooden post. Some of the neighbors painted theirs with flowers, sunsets, and even Confederate flags. Guess they want the boxes to look as nice as their lawns.

The sidewalk in front of my house is clean and smooth, not broke up like the ones on Eddie's side. We even have grass on the part next to the curb. My favorite thing about my street is the big, wide trees. Keeps the shade over me while I'm cutting the grass.

Our house is rented and small compared to the rest of the neighborhood. Most are wooden or red brick with long driveways. Little colored men holding lanterns that flank their doors. Most folks on this street don't like coloreds, but they don't seem to mind having those statues welcome folks into their homes.

In Greensboro, we had all kinds of folks visit the house we rented from Mr. Jimmy. Tenant farmers don't bother fussing over race. Green's the only color they care about.

Makes me think of my old friend Johnny Mack. He was a mulatto, a real light-colored boy. He hardly ever wore shoes, so the bottoms of his feet, they was black as night. He was all right. Maybe after integration, Eddie can be my next colored friend.

I walk into the house and drop the mail on the red-and-white checkered tablecloth. The return address on one of the envelopes reads: Montgomery County Board of Education. I want to know what's inside, but it's addressed to Mama, so I don't dare open it. I search through the cupboards for something I can slap between the last two pieces of bread in the bag when the back door creaks open and the screen slams.

Mama's home. She parks on the gravel driveway since we don't have a garage. Before we got to Montgomery, we didn't own a car, but Mama was able to get one with cheap monthly payments from a lot downtown. It's a '61 Rambler Classic in pale yellow with a convertible top.

"Well, hey there." Her words are breathless as she pulls off her sweater. "I thought I might beat you home today."

"Coach said on account of it being Friday and all, he let us go early.

Think he had something to do." I pull a saucer from the cupboard and drop my slices on it. "Did you bring anything to eat?"

Mama's happy expression falls a bit as she sorts through the mail, and I regret asking the question. She sits at the kitchen table without responding and tears open the letter from the Board of Education.

I go back to my bread and scoop out what's left of the peanut butter. I don't need a big meal, and I hope she doesn't think she needs to find me one. Sometimes I say some pretty dumb things.

"Mama, I'm sorry—"

"Not now, son," she says without looking up. "Why don't you go to your room and do your homework?" Her eyes never leave the letter, and I can only hope I'm doing as well in school as I thought.

In my room, I pull my homework from between the pages of my books and sit on the bed. I don't have a desk, just a dresser. On top, a film of dust lightens the brown paint. There's two pictures side by side —one of Mama and Melissa and one of Pa. Next to them is a tin cup with all the secret stuff I've collected over the years. It used to be Pa's cup, and he gave it to me. It was his favorite, but when I turned twelve, he said:

"A man needs something he can call his own in his own house. The women take the kitchen and most every other room for sewing or reading, and that doesn't leave nothing but the bathroom and the bedroom. This here cup is all a man's got sometimes to call his own. He can use it to drink away his worries or relax his mind. And now that you're becoming a man, you need your own cup. You take this and use it for whatever satisfies you." Then he handed it to me. "But take my advice and keep it dry, or else your wife's liable to take the broom to your head."

Pa and I laughed a good while over that conversation, and I love him more with every memory. I sure miss him. I pick up his frame and see myself in his face. I've got his ashy blonde hair, too. In this picture, his skin is a bit darker than usual. Working in the fields from dusk to dawn, the sun always left him with a good tan. I put down the photo and get back to my homework. Mama is sure to check in on me any minute.

I finish it more than an hour later, and Mama hasn't come up, so I go downstairs to see if everything is all right. In the kitchen, the letter sits next to the phone book. I walk over and see the yellow pages open to the Bs, with Board of Education circled in the middle of the list. The phone cord stretches from where it sits on the kitchen wall all the way into the living room. I start to go in, but the door is nearly closed, which is my signal not to disturb her. So I go back to the table and take a peek at the letter.

What I read, I can't believe.

My eyes water, though I don't really know why since these words couldn't possibly be talking about me. Maybe it's another Mark, and they sent it to the wrong address.

Mama bursts from the living room. I see anger in her eyes; her sweater's half off. I hold up the letter in silence. She pauses and tightens her lips like she wants to talk, but her mouth won't let her. Then comes, "I'll be right back." The door slams behind her, and the tires spin off the gravel driveway.

I slip into the kitchen chair. My hand trembles as I reread the words. When I get past the part about them kicking me out of Haley, it gets worse. No matter what it says, I know it couldn't be true. My eyes fill with tears.

"It's impossible." I say aloud to an empty room. "How can I be...*colored*?"

2

I check the window over and over. Mama must be as
confused as I am. Maybe that's why she rushed out of here. I
hope she's headed to the Board of Education and that it isn't closed
when she gets there. We need answers *today*.

Time drags on, and I'm pacing the whole while. A knock on the
front door startles me. I run there and look out the window. It's Eddie.
We were supposed to search for nightcrawlers. Seeing him upsets me,
but I don't know why. I swing the door open. I don't give him a chance
to talk.

"I—I can't go with you. I mean, I can't go tonight. Maybe we'll... I'll
see you at practice."

I push the door shut, but his hand stops it. "What's wrong?" He
frowns, and I wish I couldn't see it. I wish he would just disappear.

"Something came up, and I need to talk to my mother." Why I said
that I'll never know. My mind and my mouth won't work together.

He shrugs. "OK, well, I hope everything's cool—" I shut the door in
his face and walk back to the kitchen.

Right now I'm angrier than ever, not just about Eddie showing up,
but about how I just treated him. I run my fingers through my hair and
shake my head a few times. Nothing makes sense. I've lost control of

everything. Just as I plop back into the kitchen chair, the gravel crunches outside. I jump to my feet and swing open the back door. I hold the screen open.

"So, what happened?" Mama walks past me. "What's with that letter?"

"Come in here, Mark. I need to talk to you."

She leads me into the living room, her purse slung over her shoulder. She never brings her purse into the living room. Her eyes are glassy and red as she takes my hands in hers. She's breathless and slow to begin.

"I want you to listen to everything I'm about to say to you, and I don't want you to interrupt."

I nod, bracing for a load of bricks.

"I didn't tell you about your daddy because I, well, I never found the right time..."

Could this be? Is she confirming that letter? Was it really talking about me?

"No Mama—" I shake my head in disagreement and disbelief.

"Please let me finish..."

She squeezes her hands tighter around mine, but they feel weak. She's different somehow. I don't see her like I used to. I don't know. It's confusing. The words come from her mouth, but it's not my Mama talking. Not the honest woman who raised me.

"Once we got up here and Melissa went off to school, things were going so well, telling you didn't seem necessary. But now I realize my mistake, and all your mama can do now is say, "I'm sorry.""

I pull my hands from her grasp and stand, staring down at her.

"It's a lie. A dirty, stinking lie—" I slowly back away from her reach and rub my sleeve under my runny nose.

"Mark, your skin is white, and this was a whole new town. I had no idea anybody would find out. You must believe me—"

She's stealing from me. She's stealing my life away. Like she's just going to accept this. I cover my ears to block her voice.

"Mark listen—"

"I'm white. White, Mama, just like you. Just like Pa—"

"Mark—"

"You're not going to believe those people, are you, Mama? They hate me. They hate me because of Eddie—"

"Mark!"

"You can't let them do this. You can't."

"Mark, listen, it's gonna be all right—"

"All right?" I avoid looking at her. The air is thin, and I can't breathe being in the same room with her. I run to my room and slam the door, but I can't get the letter out of my head:

...mulatto father...

...Indiana marriage not valid in this state...

...no longer eligible to attend a white school...

None of it makes sense. I know I was born in Indiana, but thinking that far back is tough. My memory's blurry. Mama told me we didn't stay there long since Pa got a chance to work some land in Greensboro.

I sit on the bed, but just as fast, I stand again. I'm pacing. Thinking. Pacing.

I see flashes of things—the few things that I remember. A motel. I see my sister Melissa and me. We kept sneaking across the street. Colored people were over there—just colored people. The motel must have been colored. I don't know. And a juke joint. I see that too. Melissa said we used to go over there when Mama and Pa weren't around. I see shadows of people inside. Colored people. Not one white person's face comes to mind. They played music, and we danced barefoot on the dirt road until they chased us away.

If this letter is true, then I don't want to think about those days anymore or anything else that reminds me of them. Stuff gets clearer and starts to make sense, but I don't want to know. I don't want to see anymore.

Short bursts of breath come out like I'm about to choke. I feel my stomach turn, and I know I'm going to vomit. I run to the bathroom and spill out every drop of my insides. I want to puke this lie out of my life. I just want to flush the toilet and let it go.

I stay on the bathroom floor hugging the commode. It feels cold, and I'm so hot. My breath smells like a pigsty, so I get up to rinse my mouth. The mirror sees me. It sees a white boy. A WHITE BOY, NOT A COLORED BOY. My face is so red it could bleed, and I don't want to look anymore. I schlep to my room, plop face down on the bed, and wish with all my might that I could die right there.

While my face is buried in the pillow, the floor creaks outside my door. She's tapping. I ignore it.

"Mark, you let me in, you hear me?"

I don't respond. I don't ever want to speak to her again.

I know that's wrong...but I don't care.

After a while, the tapping and pleading stop. The floor creaks until the sound disappears down the stairs.

In the quiet of my room, my life story reels through my head like a moving picture. It's ruined. Forever. I roll onto my back, and my eyes fall on the picture of Pa. Everything starts to connect: How easily his skin tanned. The things he liked to eat that only colored folks ate. His friendly attitude towards them. It all starts to make sense and doesn't at the same time. None of Pa's relatives looked colored. Not the picture of Grandma he used to carry in his pocket watch, or Grandpa, who worked with us a spell before he died at 92.

So what made him colored?

I also remember Pa fighting with Mr. Jimmy over pay. He always wanted to cheat my daddy. Always treated him different. Mr. Jimmy never fought with other white farmers. And when Pa died, Mr. Jimmy didn't want to give Mama his pay. He...he knew. He knew about Pa. He *had* to know.

But why? Why didn't Pa tell me?

I breathe deep, feeling the hard frown taking over my forehead. My Pa was...colored. But I loved him. I love him. I don't have anything against him. It's Mama I can't forgive.

Pa always said raising children was women's work. Still, I wish he had told me himself. Man to man. Just him and me. I stare closer at his smooth face half covered with a light brown shadow around his mouth, over his chin, and out to both ears. His beard never grew any thicker since Mama preferred him clean-shaven. I gaze at this *colored* man.

Why isn't my Pa here when I need him?

The clock moves on. One hour. Two. I know I can't stay in bed forever. I'm hungry, and my stomach begs me to go to the kitchen. But she's there. I know it. I bet she's reading that letter—my death sentence.

I lie here all mixed up. I don't want to know the truth, but I need to know, and none of my questions will get answered in this bed.

I go downstairs, and there she is, just like I thought. I stand still until she notices me. She looks up from the letter with a face full of strength and courage, the opposite of what I'm feeling.

"What happened, Mama? Tell me...everything."

She reaches out for me, and I sit next to her. Her words hurt, like getting hit upside the head with a baseball bat. They reach into my gut and pull out everything living. No pain I've ever had hurt this much.

"...I got pregnant with Melissa in Melrose, and we wanted to marry, but whites and coloreds couldn't in the South. So we went to Indiana. There we wouldn't have to explain anything about our race. Your daddy wanted that day to be special, not humiliating.

"After you were born, we came back, but we couldn't stay in Louisiana since folks knew us. So we went to Greensboro, where nobody asked us anything. He got hired on the farm, but soon after we got there, a man who knew your daddy back in Melrose threatened to tell Mr. Jimmy. He wanted half our earnings to keep quiet. We couldn't do that, not with two kids to feed. So he told Mr. Jimmy, who started mistreating us. Then the flu came, crippling whole families. When your daddy came down with it, all I could do was pray."

Mama looks at me with sad eyes.

"Down here in Montgomery things seemed to be working out. But you can't run away from yourself, Mark. I learned that the hard way. The school board must've suspected something when they saw you were born in Indiana. We put your daddy's real race on your birth certificate. It seemed the right thing to do at the time. They contacted the marriage license place up there, and that's how they found out."

She holds her lips tight, and I know she's waiting for me to speak. So many things run through my head, but none of them matter. What's done is done.

"What happens now?" I ask in a low voice.

She looks away and puts the letter back into its white envelope.

"Forgiveness, I hope. Because there's nothing else I can say or do to make this right." She stares off to somewhere as she goes on, her fingers clasped together. "It's your choice whether you want to believe what this country says you are. It wants you to think you're less than. Less than they are, less than the world. It wants to decide what's worthy and what's true. And if you don't go along, it grabs you by the throat and chokes the self-respect out of you. Then they've won, son. They've won. What they've won, no one knows...because they're never satisfied with what they squeeze out of you...and they hate you even more for letting them do it."

Mama lowers her head and lets it slowly rest on her clasped hands.

I stand there, not knowing what to do or think or how to feel. Anything I wanted to say won't come out, and any way I wanted to respond is gone. I walk past her, open the cupboard door, and get a teacup. I go over to the stove and turn on the fire under the kettle. Then I gently rest the teacup and a small spoon in front of her. She grabs my hand and weeps. I take the blonde strands of her wispy hair and pull them delicately around her ears, the way my daddy used to do.

———

After the school board expels me, they tell Mama they won't make it public. They say they want to spare her any embarrassment, but Mama says they have other reasons.

"The county is about to get a ruling in that lawsuit against them," she says. "That colored woman, Johnnie Carr, is suing to get her son in a white school. She's likely going to win, and if she does, they'll look awful bad if the courts find out they expelled a colored kid."

I don't like the sound of being called 'a colored kid,' so I ignore that part.

"Well, why don't you tell the courts, Mama? Maybe then I can get back in?"

"I can't. I made a deal with them—"

"A deal?"

"They said they wouldn't report you as a truant as long as I got you into another school before summer." Mama sighs and rubs her forehead. "The last thing I need is them claiming I'm violating the law. I could lose my job, and though mopping floors isn't exactly the best occupation, it's paying the bills."

"But it's their fault, Mama."

She looks at me with tired eyes that are fresh out of answers. Her condition is worse lately, and I worry about how much longer she can work on her knees. The doctors say it's a blood disorder. Porphyria, they call it. Makes her insides hurt, and I can tell it's real painful, so I try not to complain, at least 'til she's feeling better.

"As long as the kids at school don't know, maybe I'll—" Then a thought makes my eyes bug out. "What am I going to do about the dinner at Billy's house Sunday?

"Calm down, Mark. Just go to dinner and don't say anything. They won't know about this. The school board promised not to announce it. You shouldn't have a thing to worry about."

———

The day of the dinner, I'm thinking about staying home. What if Billy asks me why I wasn't in school last week?

On the bright side, at least Mama's feeling better. She's fussing over my hair, my spit-shined shoes, and the suit she had cut down after Pa died. I'm jittery as a cat in a doghouse.

"What if they know already, Mama?" I say as she dusts off the back of my pants with a wet rag. "They might throw me out of the house."

Mama comes around to face me. She doesn't smile, and I know why. She's never wanted me to work. After the flu took my daddy, she didn't want Melissa and me to live the rest of our lives on a farm. Mama's trying her best, but I can't stand to see her struggle. She thought she could take care of us after Melissa went off to college on a full scholarship, which left only one mouth to feed. She wants me to focus on school, too. Sarah Lawson is a proud woman. Of course, I never ever call her Sarah, just like I never called my daddy James. Respect is real important in my family.

She wipes my face with that wet rag.

"Mama," I complain, swatting her away. She's been wiping my face since I was a baby. Makes me think she still sees me as one.

"Just mind your manners and speak when you're spoken to," she says. "And don't worry."

"I won't be able to talk. I'll be too nervous."

"Hush now and get on your jacket, or you're gonna be late."

———

Billy's house is more like a mansion. The front door is thick and wide with swanky carvings in the wood and a shiny brass knob. My skin gets clammy standing there. I'd never been inside a house like it before, and I hope my country ways don't seep out.

I pull my collar away from my neck. I'm suffocating inside my shirt and tie. I never wear them, except when Mama makes me go to church. I couldn't breathe when she tightened the bow, and now, my breath is fighting for its life. I hope that's all the fighting I gotta do in here.

I look down at my shoes. Nice and shiny, and tight too, just like my shirt. The door swings open. Billy's wide grin puts me at ease.

"Hey Lawson, come on in. Mama and Matt's waiting to meet you."

So far, so good.

The scent of baked chicken tickles my nose. My mouth waters.

Inside, I feel like I've shrunk to the size of an ant. High ceilings and long halls go from room to room. Fancy lamps sit on fancy tables with flowers or books or little statues. The windows in the supper room shoot right up to the ceiling.

"You'll sit here, next to Mama," Billy says.

A colored woman comes in and puts a big bowl of mashed potatoes on the table. She's wearin' a fancy white apron and cuffs on her pressed blue dress.

Can she tell I'm not white?

"I hope you got a big appetite," she says with a wide smile. Her teeth are as bright as her apron.

"Yes, ma'am." I say, reaching for my napkin. I search her eyes, but all I see is kindness. She disappears into the kitchen, which is when Billy's family shows up to the table.

Coach Justice catches me off guard without his uniform. Instead, he wears a dark grey suit with cuff links that sparkle like diamonds. He's got a cigar clenched between his teeth and a wrinkled newspaper in his hand. If I saw him on the street, I wouldn't know him. "So, Mark, how do you like our home?" He puts down his cigar to offer his hand. I feel weird shaking it, as if I never met him.

"I like it fine, sir."

"You're a good ballplayer, Mark. Real talent is what you've got. You have to be good at what you do. That's how you succeed."

I gulp.

He grunts at the rest of the family mulling around the room. They immediately take their places. Billy's mother sits next to me, with Billy and his older brother Matt on the other side.

Matt's a senior and the apple of Billy's eye. Though this is my first time meeting him face-to-face, it's like I already know him. Billy talks about him all the time at practice and gets nervous whenever he's in the stands. Matt's hair is slicked back like he used a whole tube of Brylcreem. He frowns at me. I clear my throat.

Mr. Justice is at the head of the table, like Pa used to be. We say the prayer, and then everyone just sits there. I figure maybe they're waiting for me, since I'm company. That's the way Pa taught me: always let company dig in first. So I reach for the mashed potatoes, but Billy's hand stops me. I sweat a bit and hope I didn't break some rule that's different from my daddy's. I hope I'm not acting colored.

"Lilly will do that," Billy says, his eyes motioning to the maid just coming out of the kitchen. "She serves us."

I sigh and put my hand down. I watch Lilly dish up the potatoes.

"More, Billy?" she asks him.

"No, but you can come back when I'm ready for seconds," he says in a serious tone. It reminds me of the field overseers we had in Greensboro. Their voices made you understand who was in charge.

As she makes her way around the table, all of them use that tone with her, but as far as I can tell, she doesn't seem to mind. Guess she's used to it.

"So Mark," says Billy's mother. "What kind of work does your father do?"

"His daddy's dead," Billy blurts.

I lower my fork and swallow. She looks pale all of a sudden.

"I'm sorry to hear that," she says. "And your mother?'

"She works at the library downtown," I say, trying to concentrate on my baked chicken.

"Is she a librarian? I didn't know they hired a new one," she says this like she's asking me to confirm it.

"No ma'am," I say, and get right back to eating.

Coach Justice gives his wife a look I'd seen my daddy give Mama when he wanted her to stop talking. In fact, everyone at the table keeps silent for about five minutes, and I know it's for my mama and me. When Mama first registered me at Haley, folks did the same thing after she told them she was a cleaning lady.

Mr. Justice opens his mouth like he wants to say something, but he doesn't. Instead, he takes a puff of his cigar, still smoldering in the ashtray next to his plate. It smells like the curing barn back on the farm.

"Got any aspirations, son, like when you grow up?" Coach Justice finally asks.

"Yes, sir," I say, glad we're off the subject of my home life. "One day I might open a baseball store to sell kids equipment and stuff, but for now, I just need an after-school job—"

I freeze right at that moment. I didn't plan for it to come out that way. I hold my fork in midair and wait for the fallout. Billy smirks at me before he stuffs his mouth with baked chicken.

"Now, Billy. Mark here might make a good businessman. In fact, that's one of the reasons I agreed when Billy asked you to join us for dinner, son." He looks at Billy. "My boy here needs some good influences in his life—"

"Aw, Pop," Billy moans.

Matt gives his father a frown. Mr. Justice points a finger at Matt. "Now you just hush up. You're gonna be grown and leaving us soon, and I want Billy to make some wholesome friendships."

If only Mr. Justice knew the truth about me.

Billy lowers his head and stuffs peas into his mouth. A few of them miss their mark and end up on the white tablecloth. Lilly comes round to pinch them up.

Coach Justice leans toward me. "You strike me as a boy who's had a good raising, and that's the kind of boy I want my Billy around. Since you're interested in business, we'd make a good match. We Justices know right much about business, as I'm sure Billy's told you. A boy like yourself could learn a lot from us."

Billy frowns, but I sit up and give a big smile, relieved I didn't blow it. Maybe things will be okay after all. Maybe my race won't matter since I still *look* white.

"Yes, sir. I sure would like to work for you all someday."

Billy coughs, and his older brother whacks his back a few times.

"So you lookin' to get a job with us?" asks Matt.

"I—I well—"

Billy pipes in. "He ain't asked for one yet, but I reckon he wants one. He gave me his Mickey Mantle. The best one." He smiles at me and forks up some mashed potatoes.

"That's serious," Matt teases. "The number one requirement for employment."

"It is in *my* book," Billy scoffs.

"Mind your manners," says Coach. "It's no secret that most of the boys on the team are working after school and on weekends for the sponsors, so why shouldn't Mark?" He turns to me. "We might be able to start you out in our new warehouse, over on Carter Hill. That's close to where you live, ain't it?"

"Y-yes, sir."

I can't believe my ears. Is he offering me a job? Looks like Mickey Mantle paid off.

"Of course, it's just a small job, sweeping floors and moving boxes. But I know from watching you on the field that you're strong enough and smart enough to manage it."

I put down my fork and give him my full attention.

"Don't forget, you gotta make practice, too," says Billy, reminding me he's the team captain. "Coach don't like it when boys work and miss practice."

I look to Coach Justice for that answer. After all, I don't know the hours or anything yet. Sweat beads form again. Then he turns to me and says, "How do you feel about coloreds, Mark? Especially our new pitcher, Eddie Goshay—"

"Dad wants to make sure you ain't no nigger lover," Matt blurts.

My eyes grow wide as saucers. Mama never allows me to say that word, and Pa hated it. He told me never to use it. My mouth is open, but nothing comes out. Mrs. Justice picks up her napkin and pats her lips.

"Ah, don't be so shocked, Lawson," says Billy. "The only folks who don't like the word 'nigger' are coloreds, and that's only because they don't want to admit what they are."

My cheeks warm after he says that. Lilly walks in and clears the dishes. I watch her silently pick up each plate and stack them in her other hand. I know she heard the conversation. Her face doesn't have any expression. Like she's invisible.

"Do you go to church, Mark?" Mrs. Justice's question snaps me out of my daze. "We're always looking for youngsters to join the choir."

I'm too mixed up to respond.

"Bring in the pecan pie, Lilly," Mr. Justice calls after the maid. "You're gonna love Lilly's pecan pie. It's the best in town."

———

That night, I dream I'm back at Haley cleaning out my locker. By the way the kids treat me, the news is out, and they sop up the gossip like biscuits and gravy.

Bosley comes over, and we just stare at each other like we never met. His eyes water, and my lips tighten. It feels strange and stupid, us just staring and not talking. Then he puts his hand on my shoulder and shakes his head, like I'd seen him do so many times before, except this time it's a different kind of shake. Not one of those "I can't believe she did that" shakes, or a "that joke was awful" shake. No, it's a "sorry this had to happen" shake.

He walks away, taking all my confidence with him. I know what he'd say if he did talk. He'd tell me we *might* still be friends but nothing like we were before, and it stings. But Bosley is one of those kids who can't be on the wrong side of things, and in Alabama being colored is wrong.

I kneel at my locker, taking things out for the last time, when I see Becky Gilmore come toward me. She's dangling an anvil over my head, asking me stuff like "What happened?" and "Are you really colored?" and "How can it be?" Then she drops it, and I'm flat as a pancake.

Meep! Meep!

She shoots down the hall like the Road Runner, laughing her fool head off. It's payback for all those marble games she lost.

I peel myself off the floor and get my stuff out of the locker in no time. The measly amount of belongings I had didn't take up a quarter of the space. As I head down the hall, I hear jeers:

"Get out of here, you coon!"

"White-faced Sambo!"

I walk faster, hoping the click of my heels drowns out the sound of their hate. My heart goes pound, pound, pound, and I'm overcome with a real dizzy feeling.

They chase me.

"Go home, nigger!"

"You ain't wanted here!"

As I run, I see Eddie in the hall.

What's he doing here?

He's laughing, almost doubling over.

I make it out the front door just in time, and I bend over to catch my breath. Before I leave school property, I look up at the stately building I'd come to love. Knowing it's not mine anymore makes my insides crumble. No more sitting with Bosley at lunch. No more pranks in the hall. No more white school. The last thing I leave at Haley High is the stench of my vomit.

I wake up drenched with sweat. Good thing the school sent my things to me in a box so I won't have to ever go back there again.

3

———————

$\mathcal{W}$e move from the house on Boultier Drive. Somebody called the landlord, and he told us to leave. Said he doesn't rent to coloreds, and even though Mama's pure white, I live with her, so she can't stay. She gets us a small apartment in Eastman, across Carter Hill Road, in the colored neighborhood. With everything that's going on, I have to miss the next few practices with the team. I can only hope they don't figure out why I haven't been around.

We didn't bring much from Greensboro, so the stuff we have to pack won't take long. Melissa is coming home to help. Everything's happening too fast—losing my school, losing the house, and on top of all that, Mama lost her job. I can't trust things anymore. I always expect something bad, and that's just what we get.

The library officials refuse to reconsider when Mama goes down there begging them not to fire her. They didn't tell her to her face either. Just like me, she gets a letter, saying she lied to them about her interracial marriage and that they can't have underhanded folks working in a respectable place like the library.

"Utilities are included as long as you have your voucher," the landlord at Eastman says. "If you lose that, you pay the full rent yourself." Mama lowers her lids and whispers, "Thank you."

I know it's killing her. She said she'd never take anything from the government, but without a job, we're stuck. She doesn't look well. Everything is falling on us at once, and I know it's wearing on her. She's lost weight. They gave us some help with food, but every time we sit down to supper, Mama just picks at it. She slides her plate in front of me.

"Here, you need your strength," she says. I worry about her, and when I tell her so, all she says is, "Your mama's fine, son. Just fine."

Having my sister here might cheer her up some. Melissa is five years older than me. She's been at Georgia State going on two years now. It's an integrated college so she doesn't have to worry about that. I'm sure Melissa knows about us, and her not telling me hurts almost as much as Mama keeping it a secret. Now that I know, I've got lots of questions.

She comes on the noon train with a church hat, a dog-eared book, and some strange comments about our race. The depot on Water Street nearly takes up three blocks of downtown. The trains roll in under an open roof.

I don't much feel like being in a crowd, so Mama goes in alone. While I wait outside, I watch the folks using the main entrance. The double doors sit right in front under a big awning that says UNION STATION. Way to the left is another door where colored folks are going in and out. It's much smaller, with no awning, but just as busy.

I glance back and forth from the main door to that other door. Through the glass of the main door, I can see Mama has collected Melissa. I watch as they come right through it, hugging and laughing.

After Melissa unpacks and settles at the apartment, we go over to the house on Boultier to get the last of our stuff. The landlord agreed to give us a few extra days so she could get here. The house has a porch folks call a wraparound. It's wide and white, with azaleas peeking through the slats. There's a swing in front, and wicker chairs on each side.

When we lived here, I liked sitting on the steps of the side porch away from the door. That was my favorite spot. If I had some serious thinking to do, Mama could still come out to sit and not break my concentration. Melissa liked porch-sitting, too. Now, she dangles her bare legs through the slats and lets her flip-flops hang on her toes. Like me, she wants to get one last memory in before we leave here, though the nosy neighbors on either side seem ready to shoo us away like pesky houseflies.

"It's nice and cool out here," Melissa says, enjoying the breeze that cuts through the scorching Montgomery heat.

I remain silent. I want to bring up the subject of us, but I can't.

She pulls her legs out of the slats and comes to sit next to me on the steps. I keep my eyes on my feet while she comments about this side of Carter Hill Road.

"All these flowers and things over here," she says. "I didn't notice too many around that apartment." She looks like she expects me to agree. Then she goes on about how unfair it is that privilege gets you things other people can't afford.

"Colored folks' homes would look this good if they had the money to buy them." All of a sudden, I don't want to talk about color, even to her. "But it won't stay this way for long. These people better wake up because a revolution is coming."

When I don't respond to that either, she gets up and walks into the yard. She bends over and picks up a broken branch, raises her arm like she's about to have a sword fight, and then pokes the air.

"Come on, Mark, let's duel like we used to when we were kids."

She prances around in a loose cotton blouse; its tassels bounce as she jabs at an imaginary me. Her blue jeans have patches sewn on and raggedy edges. Her hair is long and stringy. She's too old to play Three Musketeers, but she doesn't look it. When I ignore her, she sits next to me again and drops the stick on the step.

"It has its advantages, you know." She says this more to herself than to me. "Not many people in the world can look one way and be another..."

I heave a sigh, lean over, and pick up the stick. Now that she's brought it up, I don't know what to say, and a part of me doesn't want to say anything.

"There's this author named Nella Larson who wrote a book about it. She lived way before these days, and those people managed to do it just fine."

I don't reply. Instead, I pull the bark from the stick.

She giggles. "Oh, if you could see the looks on the girls' faces at school when they find out I'm colored. They honestly can't believe it."

The comment makes me uneasy, but I hope she doesn't notice. I keep stripping off the dark, rough surface of the stick.

"And you know the best part? Since our school is integrated, I can be whomever I want, whenever I want. It's so-o-o-o groovy."

Melissa lets out another giggle. I don't know why she's trying to make me think it's OK for her to pass for white. From some of the things I overheard on the phone, she hangs out with coloreds, too. I thought she went up to college to learn something, not put on some kind of magic act.

Finally, she turns to face me. I keep focused on the white flesh of the stick, now totally free of its dark, rough bark.

"Why do you want to resist going to a colored school? Mama told me all about it. I think it's shameful you don't want to know Daddy's people. Don't you love him anymore?"

I drop the stick and jump to my feet. I feel hot all over, and not because of the sun.

"I love Pa, and don't you ever forget it. You got some nerve accusing me when you can't even decide who *you* are. You been up at that school hobnobbing with white girls, then you're off to the Elks Club, dancing, laughing and smoking Viceroys with the coloreds—"

"What business is it of yours?" Then her eyes grow wide. "You been eavesdropping on my phone calls, 'cause I know Mama didn't tell you that."

"There you go talking country. Ain't they teaching you nothing up there?"

"Why don't you just admit it, Mark? You're ashamed of being mixed. Of being who you really are. You—you're ashamed of Daddy."

It takes everything decent in me not to whack her. But I've never hit a girl, and I'm not about to start. I squeeze my eyes shut and count to ten. When I open them, she's still there, staring at me with those beady blues.

"You act like there's nothing to it," I say. "Like you can be one thing and then another whenever you good and darn well please—like you're changing clothes or something. Just 'cause you look white don't mean you have the *right* to be white. If it was that easy, every *mixed* person would be doing it."

"So how do you think I should act, Mr. Smarty Pants? I don't see you figuring it all out. Wake up, Mark. It's about solidarity with our brothers, both black and white. Can you dig that? We don't need anyone telling us how to run our lives. We can be what we want to be. Times are changing."

She looks around and waves away the houses across the street and the nosy neighbors next door. "These people are losers, man. They're the past, and we're today."

She stands and forces a smile, then runs her fingers through my hair like she always does. I jerk my head. She shrugs, then steps off the porch and walks away. She never looks back. Something turns sour in my heart, and I know it's our relationship. Over the years, my sister has tried hard to protect me from the world. But now the world is here, and it's up to me to manage it.

———

About a week goes by, and still no word about the job from Coach Justice, so I figure I'm not getting it. I haven't seen the team since I left Haley, and I'm not looking forward to it. I go out looking for work again.

I have one last sponsor to try: Miller's Grocery. None of the guys I know work there on account of his buying uniforms for the Bloodhounds. Far as I'm concerned, the Bloodhounds are my enemies on the field, not off, and if I can get me a job, I couldn't care less if they sponsored the Dixie Hummingbirds.

Miller's store is downtown, like most of the other businesses, so I catch the bus. I stand behind a woman with a small boy struggling with a chocolate bar that's getting the best of him. White socks sit around his thick ankles like they've given up. The whoosh of air released from the brakes tells me the door's about to open.

I pay my fare and take a seat in the back. Now that coloreds can sit wherever they want, nobody's ever back here. And since nobody knows about me, I won't be bothered. I like it back here. I can watch the world out the window and daydream about what life'll be like once I'm employed…if I ever get hired.

I'm real hungry when I get to Miller's, and there's a huge stand out front with more fruits and vegetables than I've seen since we left the farm. The store itself looks empty. No one's even outside to watch over the stand, so I walk inside. Empty. Rather than wait, I go back out to the cart of apples. They shine in the sunlight, redder than a fire engine. I know I'm not supposed to steal, but no one's around, and those apples are calling me. I look around, then grab a few. I put one in my back pocket and I chomp on the other. No sooner do I have the skin of that apple between my teeth when sirens pierce my ears. A police car pulls up right in front of the store. The window rolls down, squeaking as it makes its way to the bottom. I freeze but relax again. For a minute, I forget I don't look colored.

"Come here, boy," the officer on the passenger side says. I push the apple out of my back pocket. It falls to the ground with a thud and rolls off the curb. I ignore it.

"Can't you hear?" He pushes open the car door. "I said get over here."

I'm scared a little now and go over to him, holding the other apple down close to my side. I can't bring myself to drop it. I want to finish it.

The officer stays in the car. That's when Mr. Miller comes out.

"What's all the commotion?" he asks the officer on the passenger side. The driver is colored. On the news they said the mayor had to hire some colored police on account of the Civil Rights Act.

"We caught this boy stealing," says the colored officer. He talks through the window past the white officer.

Mr. Miller eyes me. His face is soft and not the least bit angry.

"Those your pa's trousers?" he asks me. "They're kind of big, ain't they?"

I know I've lost a little weight since I left Haley, so I use a belt to keep my pants up. I didn't think it was noticeable.

"I seen you come 'round here before with your mama. She don't buy much when she comes."

I don't say anything. I'm waiting for him to tell the officer to arrest me. But instead, he waves him off.

"It's okay, Nick," he says to the white cop on the passenger side. "No harm done."

"You sure?" asks the colored officer. He seems ticked off at Mr. Miller.

"I'm sure," Mr. Miller says, ignoring him and directing his answer to Nick. "Y'all got something better to chase after than this youngster."

Officer Nick tips his hat and rolls up the window. As the cruiser pulls off, the colored cop looks like he's fussing with his partner.

"You hungry, son?"

I lower my head. "I can pay you back for this apple." I say, not knowing how I would.

Mr. Miller puts his hands on his hips. His white apron is stained and dull. His black hair is receding to the point that there's nothing in the middle. A pencil is stuck over his left ear.

"Wait here," is all he says.

I figure that means I can keep the apple, but I hurry to finish it just in case, and then I search around for the one that fell on the sidewalk, hoping he'll let me keep it, too. I don't see it, so my eyes move down the street, following the edge of the curb.

"What you looking for, son?"

I look up to see Mr. Miller holding a bag of groceries. His eyes search the concrete too, then he reaches into one of the stands to grab another apple. He drops it into the bag.

"Here." He pushes the bag into my arms. "And don't let Nick catch you stealing any more of my apples, you hear? He's not as forgiving as I am."

"Thanks, sir." I can't tell him with words how grateful I am or how happy Mama's gonna be when she sees what I brought home.

I find Mama lying down when I get there. She's been resting so much, it doesn't even seem out of the ordinary anymore. The first time I learned about Porphyria, we were still in Greensboro on the tenant farm. I came in from the fields to find her sprawled out on the floor, so

I ran fast as lightning to get help. Mr. Jimmy called the country doctor, but he didn't know what to do, so he had them take her to the hospital. They did some tests on her, and that's when we found out. Aside from being painful, the doctors say the condition makes her nervous system go haywire, especially when exposed to certain pesticides.

Sometimes she vomits and has to lie down a long time. Not much can be done about it but pain management, they say. No cure as yet. I still hope.

"Mark?" Mama calls me from her bedroom.

"Yes, Ma'am."

"Where you been so long? I was worried."

"Looking for work is all."

"Any luck?"

I really don't want to tell her, but at least I have this food.

"I went downtown to Miller's Grocery, and he had something for me to do." I lie, but it's a good lie. Besides, I did do something. I picked that apple off the ground. "Then he gave me a whole bag of groceries."

"That's wonderful." Her voice is weak but happy.

"Mama, did you have an attack today?"

She's silent for a moment.

"Just a small one," she whispers. "And don't you go worrying about it. I got along just fine."

It's not hard to tell when Mama has an attack anymore. I check the john to see if she flushed. If the water's brown, the doctor says that's a bad sign. It is brown, but I keep quiet. She's fine now and resting. I'll only upset her if I question her about it, so I flush it away.

On account of her condition, Mama can't find steady work. That's why I've got to get an after-school job. I'm a hard worker, and I'm experienced, too. On the farm, Melissa and me had lots of chores. We picked vegetables in our bare feet, up and down dirt rows that ran to the bottom of the sky. Mama and Melissa wore wide straw hats to keep the sun's glare from turning their skin to leather. We'd slave out there for hours on end, bent down 'til we could hardly stand straight.

Once Pa fell ill, our work doubled.

Mama says when new workers came down from the North to help

harvest the crops, they brought the flu with them. Mr. Jimmy kept it a secret so as not to scare off the regulars. A few other folks died, and a whole bunch more got real sick. I wish Mama hadn't told me about Mr. Jimmy's cover-up. I could never look at him straight after that. He's my enemy for life.

But the chores still had to be done if we wanted to keep eating, so I ended up doing most of the work. Every time I went looking for Melissa, she was wrapped up in some book. Sometimes I found her hiding behind a roll of baled hay. Or she'd sneak up to the barn loft and crawl way in the back. Mama always said she was extra smart and would get into college one day. That full scholarship was a blessing. We sure didn't have the money to send her.

All I can think of is that I still might have a job with Coach Justice. I pray real hard about it that night. God knows we need it. I'm not really a churchgoer, but Mama is, so I do what she tells me. She says praying helps her. I just hope He's listening. Mr. Miller's food settles my stomach so I can sleep good, but just as soon as my eyes open, it lets loose a strong, wild growl.

———

After we move, Mama gets right to work to find a school in the area that's willing to accept me as white. We turn so many Yellow Pages I can feel heat on the tips of my fingers. After a couple of days, we find a few schools, but every time she calls or visits, she hears only, "No." This continues for two weeks. It doesn't matter to them if I'm three-quarters white, half white, or any part white. My father was mulatto, and that ends the conversation.

It's crystal clear that my smidgeon of blackness is shutting the door to every white school within fifty miles. Of course, a few of the integrated schools in other towns will have me, but we'd have to move, and I definitely don't want to leave my ball club.

"The local school board is standing firm. Until they come up with the desegregation plan the courts just ordered, they're not taking in any colored students." Mama explains it all to me while we sit at the kitchen table. She's drinking her favorite hot tea, and I'm taking my time with some chocolate milk.

"You're fourteen, so you wouldn't be eligible for that Freedom of Choice program, and even if you were, we already missed the April first deadline..."

I pick up the letter that's still sitting on the kitchen table: April 3, 1966.

What a con. They knew I wouldn't qualify before they even sent it.

She says Freedom of Choice is supposed to help integration by letting the high school kids choose where they want to go. Deadline or not, most coloreds who asked to go to a white school didn't get in. She says the board tells colored students that the school they want to attend is overcrowded or some other excuse to keep them out.

I take a deep breath, knowing this is going to be a lot harder than I thought.

Mama lowers her eyelids. She's running her finger alongside her teacup.

"On account of the lawsuit, they were forced to take one or two colored children, but word is, most of the white parents are doing everything they can to get rid of them." She looks up from her tea. The steam swirls around the rim and disappears into the air.

"I overheard some women talking at the doctor's office," she goes on. "They even want to cancel the prom so those few coloreds can't go."

A dance. I won't be able to go to one of those this year, that's for sure.

"What about the new school? Jefferson Davis. I could go there."

"Honey, Jeff Davis won't be finished this year. We'll keep looking."

I abandon my milk and take my disappointment to the fire escape. It don't compare to the fancy porch on Boultier—but it's big enough for thinking. While I wait for a decision from the remaining schools, I spend a lot of time alone. The guys must be wondering what gives by now. Bosley's been calling. Coach, too. I don't come to the phone. I tell Mama to say I got the flu or something. Anything but the truth.

Most days I leave the house around seven in the morning while Mama is still asleep, then I head over to the golf course. Since no one can tell my race, they don't stop me. It's the one place even some white people can't join. You have to have money, but they don't mind me hanging over by the pond as long as I don't get in the golfers' way. They don't tee off until eight or nine sometimes.

I squat at the edge of the water and sit real quiet. I listen, trying to make out every sound. Birds chirping. Bees buzzing. Sometimes while I sit, I feel helpless inside. It pushes its way up through my chest and into my throat. I heave and sniff and finally let it out. My bawling gets so loud it scares the birds. It doesn't last long though, and I'm back to just sitting. I'm not a big baby, but if I'm gonna cry, this is a good place to do it.

I usually feel better after I go there, but when I get home one morning, all that changes. I walk into the house and see schoolbooks on the kitchen table, and one of them says *The History of the Negro in America.*

"It's no use," Mama sighs. "There's nothing available. You'll just have to go to Douglass."

I panic.

"Douglass?"

"Mark, listen to me—"

"I can't go there."

"School's almost out, honey. It'll only be for a month—"

"No."

"You've got to go to school, Mark, or you'll be a truant."

"That's it? You're just gonna let me go to Douglass?"

She might as well have enrolled me in prison.

Mama stands with her hand on her hip. I can see in her face she doesn't want to go any rounds with me, like I'm Cassius Clay. In her eyes she looks defeated.

"Why, Mark?" She starts in almost a whisper. "Why are you making this so hard? Your daddy fought against racists all his life, in Louisiana and Greensboro." The more she talks, the louder and angrier she gets. It's not like her. She paces, wringing her hands. "It never stops...this hate. And you're acting just like them...you're acting just like a little racist!"

A racist?

I keep a tough look on my face but soon feel it crack into sadness. That's when she cups her hands over her mouth like she wishes she could take it back. Tears swell, but I'm too angry to let them out. I stomp down the hall, holding back until I get to my room. I can hear Mama come behind me, but I slam the door.

"I'm sorry, Mark. I'm so sorry. I'm tired, and I...I'm so, so sorry..."

As I lie there, I can hear her whimper outside my door. I ignore her until she goes away. I don't mean to hurt her, but what she did hurt me.

It's like a nightmare that never ends. If I knew a long time ago, I could have gotten used to being with coloreds. I'd probably not even want to be around white people. Maybe I'd even feel like Eddie. Though I can't really imagine that, and that's the problem. I don't know how to be around colored kids. I played with them on the farm, but I never was friends with them. Never shared secrets with them or made pacts with them or anything. Except Johnny, but to me, he wasn't really colored. He was white as me.

That's when going to Douglass sets in.

What do colored kids do in school? Winston told us he heard the teachers at the colored schools cook collard greens and pig's feet and make the kids eat them. And Ray said they don't have a real gym, so they play all their games on a dirt floor. Of course, Billy always says they don't do anything but put on minstrel shows. I kind of believe that's a lie since Eddie says they do learn stuff, even though it's mostly about colored people.

What if they don't teach anything about white people?

I put my hands over my eyes and try not to think about it anymore. Then all of a sudden it hits me: If I go to Douglass, I'm going to be the only white kid in there—the only one. I could get jumped after school, or maybe the teachers will let the kids do it right there in class. Maybe they don't even have rules about stuff like that.

Can colored people lynch white people?

If they do, they might go to jail after I'm dead, but they'd probably be glad to get caught so they could brag about finally killing a white boy. 'Course, the truth is, I'm not white anymore. Even though I look white, I'm not.

Those kids won't care. They won't accept me as "a brother," like the coloreds around here call each other. And I don't want to be one.

I don't care what Melissa's doing at school. I'm not going to be two races. I'm going to be one—the right one. The only one that's going to get me a good job. I'm going to be the one people see when they look at me. The one I've always been.

4

———————

*M*ama once told me a story from the Bible about a kid named Daniel walking into a lion's den. That's how I feel walking toward the entrance to Frederick Douglass High.

I can't stop my chest from heaving in expectation...of what I don't know. I'd seen white kids jump colored kids before, but never the other way around. I hope they don't make this difficult, though I'm not dumb enough to think I can come into their territory, expecting a cheesy smile, a tap dance, or anybody offering me some "skin."

I keep my eyes peeled as I walk, like I'm a pitcher, ready to turn and throw, knowing someone's trying to steal second base. They stand their ground as I pass. Staring eyes. Some mean, some questioning. One boy steps in my path. I don't flinch. He backs down, laughing.

"Hey," a voice behind me says. I'm not sure who it's talking to until the boy comes around to face me. His skin is nearly as white as mine. He sticks out his hand. I look at it but don't take it. He pulls it back to his side.

"I'm Philip Johnson. You must be the new kid they've been talking about."

He's smiling but not in a sneaky way. I let out some of my captive air.

"I'm Mark Lawson," I say, trying to return his politeness.

"Hey Mark, nice to meet you."

He looks out at the other kids standing on the cement steps of the entrance. They go on about their business. I wonder what they've been saying about me.

"Come on. I can show you around."

I walk with Philip up the steps, past the mean and questioning eyes, and into the building.

"It's tough being new here, but you'll get used to it."

As we walk down the hall, I watch Philip. Part of me still thinks he could steal second. He's about my height, with straight, brown hair but thick, like the Beatles. He has on a button down shirt under a blue sweater vest. He must be a sophomore. He looks older than me.

He takes me on a tour, starting with the office, then into the gym, and finally, my least favorite place: the cafeteria. The rooms are a lot smaller than at Haley and not half as nice. Then there's the problem of Eddie. I don't look forward to running into him at this school.

Philip and I make small talk, like where we live, and our favorite subjects. When he brings me back around to the office, he says, "So what's it like to be colored at a white school?"

My eyebrows knit.

"I knew you were colored the minute I saw you," he says. "We can recognize each other."

I'm confused and I'm sure I look it.

"Oh, I guess you didn't think anyone knew," he says, turning to watch the kids now filling the hall. "They're staring at you because they think you're here for some sort of reverse integration, since Lanier had to take Arlam Carr."

"Who?"

"The boy who got into Sydney Lanier High." Philip says this like he's shocked that I don't know something he thinks is important. "I know you heard about his mother taking the schools to court, so all the kids here think that's why you came to Douglass. Like an exchange or something."

"I did hear about that kid." I admit, though I didn't know all the details. I'm sure Philip does. There's so many high schools in town, it's a wonder he can keep up with what's going on outside of his own school.

"Like I said, I knew you were colored. All light-skinned people can spot other light-skinned people, no matter how pale they are—the way your features look or something in your eyes gives you away." He says this like he's proud of this ability to single me out. "My ancestors were slaves, of course, but I guess something happened back down the line because my whole family is light."

His eyes sparkle, as if this news somehow makes us blood brothers. But I keep my mouth shut. I don't know this boy from Adam, or why he's telling me his business. Then he leans close to me, and whispers.

"They'll call you red bone or bright skinned but just ignore it. Most times their anger is really jealousy. They all want to be like us, you know." He looks at his Timex watch. "Gotta go. I'll try to find you at lunch, if we don't end up having classes together."

The bell rings and Philip takes off, leaving me standing in the hall, alone. I decide I don't want to spend time with a kid who thinks he's better than somebody of his own race. Then Eddie's face flashes in my mind. It tries to sting my conscience, but I don't let it. I head into the office to get my schedule.

I sit in one of the hard, wooden chairs and wait for the secretary to pay me attention. "Mr. Hayes will be out to see you shortly." she says.

I settle in. I figure it's going to be a long wait and hope I don't get another hunger headache. I woke up with one and Mama hadn't left any breakfast. I found a banana, but it wasn't enough.

The office doesn't impress me. It has a big glass window out front like at Haley, but no decorations celebrating school spirit. No flowers on the secretary's desk. The loudspeaker on the ceiling reminds me of an old radio Pa had in Greensboro. It had a net in front that was torn from being dropped so many times.

At least this school's clean. They probably have lots of maids and janitors willing to work on it extra hard.

"Hello, young man." says the man with close-cut hair who must be Mr. Hayes. He's dark-skinned in a dark blue suit, with a blue and gold tie—my new school colors. "Welcome to Frederick Douglass High."

"Yes, sir," I say, not as happy as I could have. His expression tells me he understands.

"I've got your information right here, but we can go over that later. I assume you've received your books?"

"Yes, sir. When we registered."

"Good. Now, why don't you and I take a walk? I'd like to talk to you." Mr. Hayes leads me out of the office, and we stroll down the hall. He tells me about the history of the school:

"...built in 1865 as a primary school,"

"...became a high school in 1956,"

"...named for Frederick Douglass, the politician and journalist. He's the one who coined the phrase, 'Power concedes nothing without a demand. It never has, and it never will."

I squint.

"Well..." says Mr. Hayes, "we also have an underground tunnel—"

"Really?"

"Sure do. We built it to connect this side of the campus with the other side."

"Can I see it?" I ask him, thinking maybe there's something cool about this place I can brag on whenever the guys at practice tease me. But I don't get too excited. I don't want Mr. Hayes to think I plan to stick around long enough to graduate.

The tunnel turns out to be nothing special. It's just an underground hallway. Down there Mr. Hayes stops to lean against the wall. His face is serious all of a sudden. He crosses his arms, which is never a good sign, especially when adults do it.

"Besides your being new to a colored school, you may also notice a difference in how our classes are taught."

"What do you mean, sir?"

"We want our students to be active learners and shape and form their knowledge. So we've adopted a teaching method based on the research of a man named Jerome Bruner..."

I blink and wonder if he expects me to know this Bruner person. Mr. Hayes smiles with eyes calm and patient.

"Jerome Bruner is a respected psychologist with a keen interest in the state of education today."

"Uh, OK."

Mr. Hayes pats my shoulder with his right hand, then directs me to go ahead of him with his left.

"It's my belief that this method of Bruner's will encourage our students to come to their own conclusions based on the information presented. We don't want you to just memorize things by rote, but rather help you put the pieces together." He winks. "I think you'll like it."

I shrug as we continue to walk through the tunnel. It's longer than I thought.

"Look, Mark, I know you don't want to be here, and I understand, but I need you to give it a shot. We're not a bad school, though we don't have all the things you were used to at Haley. We house all the post-elementary grades here, so you'll see seventh through ninth graders as well as the older students. But we strive to be a family. We look out for one another, and I hope you decide you want to be a part of that family, too."

I keep my head down the whole time he's talking because I was taught to be respectful of adults, no matter their color. But inside, I want to scream and run out of this place. I want my old life back. I breathe hard as he talks, hoping to keep my feelings under control.

"As for your classes, you'll have your first with Miss Alice May. She's firm but fair. And she doesn't 'take no mess,' from what I hear." He smiles when he says this, but I don't respond. "If there is anything I can help you with during your transition, don't hesitate to ask for permission to come to my office. I'll try to make myself available." He puts his hand on my shoulder. "And Mark, like the Good Book says, this too shall pass."

"Yes, sir."

Back at the office, he hands me my schedule and directs me to Miss Alice May's class.

"Have a good day, son."

I watch Mr. Hayes walk down the hall. His stride is confident—not at all like some of the colored men I knew in Greensboro. Guess he's one of that new breed everyone's talking about. The ones who are beginning to call themselves Black. The ones white people call uppity.

The door opens.

"Come in, young man; you don't need an invitation."

The kids snicker, but not too loud, and I remember what Mr. Hayes said about Miss Alice May not taking no mess.

"Now quiet down, everyone. I want you to meet Mark Lawson. He's going to be in this class, and I want you all to treat him the way I expect you to treat each other, and how is that?"

They all yell out. "With respect." Miss Alice May smiles.

"Good. Now Mark, you can take a seat in that row over there, behind Elizabeth. And the rest of you open your science books to page 297."

The desk and chair are wooden but not much different from the metal one I had at Haley. There's a blackboard up front, and the floor isn't dirt. Miss Alice May wears pearls, a skirt, a blouse, and a sweater over it. She looks like a regular ole teacher to me, except she's colored.

So far, the guys are wrong, though I won't know for sure until I go to lunch and see what kind of food they're serving.

The kids who sit around me are all different shades of colored. I never understood how they could all be colored when some are real light, like Philip, while others are dark. One boy in this class is so black he could be from Africa. 'Course, they're all from Africa. At least that's what I was taught. Seeing all these shades makes me wonder.

White people are pretty much all the same shade. Some are redder than others, but still white. "White" and "Black" are the wrong words. Nobody's truly white or black. Well, that kid by the window is pretty dark, and I remember a lesson on albinos last year. They're actually white. So other than that, most people aren't black or white.

None of the kids look at me during class, and I get the feeling the teacher told them not to. But nobody said I couldn't look at them. The girl in front of me, Elizabeth, has three thick braids. I lean forward, but just a little, so I can take a look without drawing attention. I never got too close to colored girls on the farm. I always wondered why their hair wasn't smooth and straight like white girls. Her braids look like they could bust apart any minute. I wonder what kind of comb could keep it all laid down. Her dress is pink and white. The bright colors look extra bright next to her skin, which is brown as a Moon Pie and just as smooth. She acts normal, though. Just sits up straight and keeps her eyes on the board or on Miss Alice May.

There's a boy on my right using his pencil to carve something into his desk. He's dark, too, but a shade lighter than Elizabeth. His pants are held up with suspenders and his sneakers look older than mine. I'm sure a barber got to him not long ago 'cause he's clean-cut.

The kid on my left keeps staring out the window like he's looking for someone. When his eyes catch mine, they bug out. He makes a face that tells me I better keep my looks to myself. Most of the kids seem to pay attention to the teacher and don't act up like I was expecting.

———

Once it's lunchtime, I see cafeteria ladies with white uniforms and nets on their heads serving up the usual school grub. Nothing much different here either, except a lot of kids use lunch tickets. The tables aren't metal like at Haley, and the benches aren't attached. They're just tables and chairs. As I pass each of them, I see milk cartons, sandwiches from home, apples, and trays. The trays hold today's lunch menu: mashed potatoes, some kind of meat with gravy on it, and corn. Same thing they served at Haley. No pig's feet or collard greens—at least not yet.

I sit alone at my table. It's way in the back, like at Haley, but this one sits near the door. When I spot Philip, I get up and take my paper bag outside. I don't want to eat lunch with him. I don't stay outside for long. The boys are playing a game that I don't: basketball.

The back of the school is pretty much a parking lot, with a field of patchy grass and a basketball hoop that looks like a torn spider web. I never learned to play, but watching the boys on my first day, I know I'm gonna be challenged. Sports is a man's calling card, and since there's no baseball field, my card's worthless. I've never seen Eddie play basketball. Maybe if you're colored, you don't have to know how. I soon discover that being *half* colored means I better learn.

"Who got next?" A sweaty boy says to anyone on the sidelines. Some boys answer by pulling off their T-shirts and throwing their caps on the ground.

"You playin'?" The sweaty boy asks me. I recognize him from Miss Alice May's class. His name is Parker. Something Parker. In class the teacher uses last names.

"He can't play no ball," another snarks. "He's a white boy."

My heartbeat quickens. Knowing this day would come, I'd been practicing what I'd say to them. But at this moment, my mind's completely blank.

"Here, take it to the hoop, whitey."

Sweaty boy bounces the ball at me. My first reaction is to sidestep it, and I let my legs carry me back into the cafeteria and away from what could turn into a bad situation. Laughter and teasing follow me inside, but ignoring it is my only option.

To avoid a fight, I don't go outside over the next few days, but after a while I get tired of hiding. Sweaty boy sees me but doesn't ask me to play. Now I just watch and see if I can learn.

After lunch, I have Mr. Jordan, who teaches history. Today it's black history.

"Turn your books to page 416." He sits wide-legged on the desk with a ruler in his hand. He doesn't use it on anybody; he just holds it all the time. "We are going to compare and contrast the Negro's role in the Revolutionary War with that of white Americans."

I stare at Mr. Jordan and wonder, *What Negro role?*

Mr. Jordan smiles at me as if he knows what I'm thinking: that at Haley, I didn't learn what he's about to teach.

"From your assignments, can anyone tell me who James Armistead was?"

"A soldier," says one girl.

"Yes," says Mr. Jordan, "but what *kind* of soldier?"

His eyes search the room. "Linda?"

"He was a spy."

"That's correct. But tell me this: Was he free or a slave?" Mr. Jordan points to a kid behind me.

"A slave, but his master allowed him to join the army."

None of this is making any sense to me, so I raise my hand.

"You have something to add, Mark?"

"Uh, no sir. I just want to know, why would a slave want to fight for a country that made him a slave?"

"Very good question. Class, can anyone answer Mark's question?"

A twinge of pride hits me, so I sit up a little. Several kids raise their hands.

"John?" Mr. Jordan says, pointing his ruler.

"Well, uh, because it was better than picking cotton?"

The room fills with laughter. Mr. Jordan smiles, shaking his head like he's in on the joke.

"John makes a good point," Mr. Jordan says. "It was a way for Armistead to escape the chains of slavery, but many slaves who were able to join the armed forces at that time in history did so for another reason. Philip?"

"If he did good in the war, then they might free him."

"Exactly. But did they always get what they were promised?"

All the kids shake their heads.

"True. In fact, most went right back to the master to slave for him once again."

I look over at Philip. He's not older than me after all. His eyes catch mine, and he smiles.

Mr. Jordan points the ruler at Philip. "Now, tell me a little more about this spy business. Who did Armistead spy on?"

"The British."

"But how?"

Mr. Jordan lets everyone answer, even if they get it wrong, and he doesn't look at us like we're stupid either. I like that.

"How about you, Mark? Did you read the assignment?"

"Uh, I—uh. I guess I missed that part."

Laughter bursts out again.

"That's enough."

Now Mr. Jordan points his ruler at me. "I know you're new here, Mark, but we all participate. I don't expect this to happen on your next assignment, OK?"

"OK."

He gives me a salute. Now I feel bad that I didn't read the book. I guess I didn't think I'd have to answer any questions, being new and all. But I do like Mr. Jordan's way of teaching, so I listen harder.

"Cassandra, what kind of spy was James Armistead?"

"He pretended to be a runaway slave, spying on the Americans. And that's how he found out stuff about what the British were doing."

"Excellent."

I raise my hand.

"Yes, Mark?"

"I, well. My teacher at Haley never said anything about slaves fighting in the Revolutionary War." I don't mean to doubt him, but how do I know he's telling us the truth?

Mr. Jordan leans back and crosses his arms.

"Would you like to tell the class what your teacher *did* say about it?"

I look around before I answer, and I don't want to sound stupid.

"Well, I don't remember all of it."

Laughter erupts.

"Settle down." Mr. Jordan tells the class, and he looks back at me. "Why don't you just tell us what you *do* remember, Mark?"

I close my eyes tight, knowing I just got myself into a pickle I might not be able to get out of, but I go for it. After all, anything I learned at Haley is probably stuff they don't even know. "My teacher, Mrs. Bennett, said that George Washington was a great military leader."

Mr. Jordan smiles. "To be honest, Mark, before he led the band of untrained, unskilled men he had to work with, he'd never commanded a large army in his life."

All the kids are murmuring now. But I'm not through yet.

"Well, she also said that all the colonists supported the war and wanted the British to stop taxing them." I sit back and smile.

Mr. Jordan gets up and walks the room. "According to the facts, Mark, less than half the colonists supported the war. There's even one account of a tavern owner who sent someone outside to look down the road every once in a while to see which side was headed his way, and then he'd throw his support behind that side, or whoever was winning. Some of the colonists even fought for the Redcoats."

More laughter. Now I'm hot under the collar.

"Maybe I just didn't hear her right, but I know we learned a lot about it," I say in a grumpy tone.

"Sometimes the facts, young man, depend on who is telling them." He smiles at me. "Remember, class, the mind that knows is the mind that grows. We'll wrap this up on Monday. Class dismissed."

Just about all my classes are like that, and after a few weeks of frustration, I settle in at Douglass. Sometimes I still get stares, and some kids call me "whitey," but I ignore it like Philip told me to. It's still taking me a while to get used to drinking from the water fountain, but other than that, it's OK. I just need to get through the next month. I don't plan to come back to this school next year. I'll get my Freedom of Choice form in early.

———

I guess Mama's getting sick of me moping around the house 'cause that Saturday she gives me a dollar and sends me off to the Paramount. It's one of the local movie theaters. Not the one the kids all cram into on the weekends. I made sure of that. In line, I keep my eyes peeled for anybody who might know me, especially anybody from Haley or even my team. Saturday's the worst day of the week if you want to hide from other kids.

At the concession stand I'm antsy. There's a big guy with his son behind me, so I use them as a shield. I wear a cap I held onto that belonged to Pa. It's bigger than my head. I also pull up my jacket collar. Good thing it's cool in here.

After getting my popcorn, I walk down the dark aisle and keep my head low to follow the little lights on each side. I take a seat way in the back and sink down.

Once the projector gets going, I lose myself inside Batman's world. Nobody's ever made a movie from the comic book before, and I nearly spill my popcorn with every whap and zap that fills the screen.

When the lights come up, I sit for a while and smile. Mama always knows how to make me feel better.

It takes a minute to get out of the place, what with all the little kids

and fussing parents, and I almost reach the exit door when I hear.
"Mark? Mark, is that you?"

A film of sweat covers my entire body. The voice. It's the last voice I
want to hear.

She bops me on the back of my head—the usual Becky greeting.

"H-hey Beck. How's tricks?" I know I sound nervous, and by the
way she narrows her eyes, she knows I am.

"Skipping school these days? Everybody wondered where you
been. And what's with the getup?"

I step out of line and station myself against the black wall, away
from the EXIT sign. She follows me. Lies of all shapes and sizes jockey
for first place in my mind.

I got an incurable disease and can't come back

*My sister dropped out of college and we had to go to Georgia to talk some
sense into her*

*My mama's sister's long-lost aunt is in town, and she's a teacher, so I
stayed home and had classes with her.*

Every lame excuse in the book sounds just as lame when I think of
it. I hate it when somebody puts me on the spot.

"Well?" Becky's not one to get off a subject until she rides it to
death, so I tell her the only thing I figure she might believe.

"We, my mama I mean, decided that since integration is coming,
and she doesn't want me going to school with coloreds, she put me in
a private school. You know? One of those Catholic ones way, way
uptown."

I take in a deep breath and give her a smile, hoping it'll seal the
deal.

Becky crosses her arms, and I know she thinks I'm fibbing.

"Really? Well…"

Here it comes. She's gonna call me out and say she knows all about
my getting kicked out of Haley and that I'm not white anymore. I
brace myself, waiting for her to blow up the bomb that's ticking inside
me. I'm clammy again. Even my toes sweat—that anvil in my dream's
about to drop for real.

"…you could've at least told somebody. Winston and Boz come

asking me about you, and I didn't know either. Some kind of friend you are, Mark Lawson."

I can hear the angels sing after that. All the heat in my body simmers to a cool ninety-eight-point-six.

"Sorry, Beck. I, I guess it all happened so fast I, I didn't have time to tell nobody."

My eyes dart around the now empty room. I perk up. "Well, the movie's about to start again, so we better get out of here. Tell everybody I said hey."

I turn to leave, but she grabs my arm.

"I hear they can still take coloreds at some of those private schools. Which one do you go to?"

"Tickets, please," says the usher who saves my life.

"We were just leaving," I say. "Bye, Beck."

I tip my hat and skedaddle just as fast as my feet'll carry me.

5

____

oach Collier is still calling—to check on me, he says, and I wonder if he knows. Says I need to get over whatever it is I got real quick 'cause the team needs me. That makes me feel good, but the reality doesn't. I wish I could get *Lost in Space* like Will Robinson. If I could, I'd never come back to Earth, and my ills would be over.

Trouble is, I can't put it off any longer. For one, I'm getting rusty, and two, I've got to be ready for the state championship.

I take my time getting to Huntingdon College. I make my way onto the long field and up to the fence. I'm not close yet, but I can see the old gang huddled together by the bench. Bosley is with them, and a chill of shame shoots through me.

I also see a few kids I don't recognize. They must be the new alternates Coach Collier mentioned on the phone. One of them is colored. I go speak to him. Since he doesn't know me, he might talk to me.

"Hi," I say to him, still looking around to see if anyone's noticed I'm here.

"Hi, I'm Peter. Who are you?" He's skinny with long, dark arms. Guess that makes it easy to catch high-flying balls. He says he goes to

Charles Drew High, the other colored school. It's still in the league's jurisdiction, so he can play on our team.

"I'm Mark. I play shortstop."

"Oh-h-h," says Peter with a laugh. "You must be the white boy who turned Black." He's reaching for my hand, but I'm not offering it.

Doggone it. Everybody must know.

"It's cool, man. I get it," he says. "You ain't used to being called black yet, but you better *get* used to it." He says this while eyeing me up and down.

"It's none of your business," I say, and push past him. I can hear him laughing behind me.

"Come on, man," he says to my back. "I ain't your enemy, unless you make me one." I turn to face him. He sure is bold for a colored kid. "I'm the first base alternate..."

He talks like I'm interested in hearing why he's here. I really don't care.

"...but I don't expect to be sitting on the sidelines for long, no sir. I'm gonna take the position from that kid over there."

He points to Ray, and my eyes grow wide. Peter's kind of brave too, or maybe he's just dumb.

"Well, uh, welcome to the team," I say.

When I get over to the bench, I see Eddie on the pitcher's mound. It's the first time I've seen him since I slammed my door on him. I swallow hard. When I get up closer, the guys look down at their feet. Some look away. Bosley says 'hi,' and that gives me some courage. A couple of others speak too, but sorta low. Most just stare. Billy looks like he ate something that didn't agree with him.

I drop my bag onto the bench, and when I turn around, he hauls off and hits me. Square in the face. Next thing I know, I'm on the ground tussling with him. I can't think. I give swings. Land blows. Tear at his hair. Yank anything I can grab. His uniform is ripped. There's dust. Blood. Coach Collier pulls me off. Winston and Coach Justice grab Billy. We breathe heavy. Me most of all.

"You dirty nigger. You knew you was black, but you came to my house. You ate my food." Billy spits at me. "My daddy ain't givin' you no job 'cause you're a nigger, just like him." He points at Eddie. That's when Peter runs toward Billy.

"Who you calling a nigger, you peckerwood?" He stands close to Eddie like they're kin.

"That's enough," Coach Collier warns.

My chest heaves, and I wrangle with Coach's grip. I want to get at Billy and bust his chops.

"I ain't no nigger," I scream. "I'm as white as you."

"Then why'd they kick you out of school?" Hank blurts. The other boys mumble.

A sense of helplessness washes over me, but I fight it with all my might. Like a wild colt, I still pull and tug to get free of Coach.

"Settle down, son," he says.

He motions to Coach Justice to take the boys to the bench. My eyes follow Billy's dad, eager to get his attention, but he never looks my way.

Eddie walks toward me, slowly, like he needs to watch his step. As he gets closer, I give him the meanest glare I can muster. The last thing I need is a colored boy feeling sorry for me.

He gapes like he's not sure who I am.

"Go over to the cage," Coach Collier tells him. "Get that arm limbered up."

When Eddie leaves, Coach looks at me sideways. He lifts the brim of his cap.

"I'll be doggone. You don't look a bit colored to me, son. But I ain't your judge; I'm your coach, so you take my advice. Be real careful. You get my drift?"

I don't even listen. All I know is I just lost my whole future, so what's the use in sticking around? Instead of joining my teammates, I walk back the same way I came. I can hear some of the boys on the field razz me.

"Mark! Come back here, boy."

It's Coach Collier calling. He runs to me and hands me my glove. "Just play ball and stay out of Billy's way. Can you do that for me?"

I agree to play even though my gut's telling me to go home. But I need to work off my anger. I walk onto the diamond like a stranger. I

can sense their eyes on me. I can feel their thoughts. I take my position
at shortstop. Ray grazes me as he walks to first. The two of us used to
taunt the batter together. With Eddie, we're supposed to be the triple
threat against Bixal. Not anymore.

The batter hits the ball high into midfield.

"Get him out," one of the players screams as the batter makes his
way toward first.

"Throw it. Throw it," I yell to the outfield. The batter's moving off
first and coming my way. Ray catches the ball from the center fielder,
but then he just stands there holding it with his arm swung behind his
head, like it's stuck.

I can see his eyes darting back and forth between Eddie and me.

"Throw the ball," I yell again as the batter hits the second base bag
and heads toward me. The batter shoves me down and slides to third. I
scurry up from the dust and snatch my glove off the ground.

So this is the way it's gonna be.

In an hour or so, things settle down—not back to normal, but
enough to finish practice. I take a squat on second and keep my eye on
the ball I'm tossing into the air and dropping into my glove. I keep
tossing it up and dropping it until everybody's gone.

I rub my hand over my face. Even though the sky is grey, there's a
stretch of pale peach on the edge of the earth. It reminds me the sun is
shining somewhere.

I pull my knees up and wrap my arms around them. A cool
breeze comes along, so I close my eyes and let it blow over me,
through my hair, and into the short sleeves of my uniform. All of a
sudden I ache. I'm bruised in all the places where Billy's punches
landed. My lip stings, too. I touch it. I feel dried blood, and it's
swelled a little.

Coach Collier offers to take me home, but I refuse, so he leaves after
I convince him I can get there on my own. I want to be alone.

I watch Eddie when he leaves the field. He keeps looking back at
me, but he doesn't say anything.

I get myself up and pull my glove off. It hurts a little to stand after
sitting so long. I stretch and look around, and then I see him. Running
toward me. Eddie's coming back. I tense up, ready to fight. But when

he slows to a stroll, I know he doesn't mean me any harm. If he did, he'd kill me; I'm so worn out.

"You headed home?"

It's a question I don't expect, so I don't allow myself to relax. "Why?"

He lowers his head and starts to leave. I'm relieved. To be honest, I don't want to fight him. I just want him to go away.

All of a sudden, he turns around, like some force is inside him, and the next thing I know, his long, black finger is right between my eyes.

"You ain't my friend," he shouts. "I thought you was, but you ain't. Why you tryin' so hard to be white if you ain't white? You know how Billy is. He played you like a piano. Why you still want his friendship knowing he hates us?" His trembling lips hesitate. He wipes away the spit. "He didn't care nothin' about you when he thought you was white, and he don't care nothing 'bout you now...whatever you are."

He says that last part looking me up and down, like he's not sure who I am. He starts to walk away, his finger still pointing at me. "You keep it up, you hear? See what it gets you."

My mouth must have been hanging open for a while. I don't even notice it until he's out of sight.

I slam my glove to the ground. The ball rolls along and comes to rest under the bench. As I leave the field, I know that from here on out I'm on my own and nobody cares. I'm like a man on a boat in the middle of the ocean who can never go home again.

———

Nothing good is coming out of this new life I'm forced to lead, but Mama is making the best of it due to the kindness of strangers. Since she lost her job, she's been getting visits from a few colored women. She says they're maids she met at the library.

"They'd talk to me when they came in to check out books for their employers' children," she tells me, "real nice ladies."

Most times when the women come to visit, they leave baskets of food for us. Good food, like greens full of spices, vinegar, and pork. Golden fried chicken that crunches when I bite into it, and the sweetest, moistest cakes I've ever tasted. The buttery flavor just melts in my mouth. I remember what Winston said about colored schools. If the food tastes like this, I might learn to like it.

The maids' generosity lasts a few days, but then we're back to scrounging.

After a while, Mama's odd jobs come along a lot less often than we need them. She's been out looking for work every day this week, and each time she comes home, she has less and less to talk about. I hope she finds something soon. We're getting more letters in the mail with doctors' names on them. I don't ask about it. I don't want her to think I'm worried, even though I am.

Mama left some of the maids' charity on the table—cans of beans, some potatoes and carrots, and cereal. I usually leave it for her to put away, but today I help out. The cupboards in this apartment are pretty small compared to the house on Boultier, but it doesn't matter since we don't eat as much. We don't qualify for much in the way of food stamps since there's only the two of us.

Our apartment is on the parking lot side of the building. Makes it easy to watch for her. I don't trust the men I see hanging around out there.

I'm reaching to the top shelf of one cupboard. There's a truck outside. From the rumbling noise it's making, it sounds like a pickup— one of those old ones overdue for a new muffler.

I don't bother to turn around until a voice rises up and I figure it's that colored woman downstairs, fighting with her boyfriend again. But for some reason the voice sounds too familiar. Not like that woman's at all. I turn away from the cupboard and stand still, holding a box of cornflakes, listening. The voice isn't the colored woman's. It's Mama's.

I go to the window, and she's standing by the car door arguing with a man who is moving quickly around a truck that says ACME Towing. He heads for the driver's side of Mama's car.

I run out of the apartment, jumping stairs as fast as I can. We're on the second floor, so it doesn't take me long before I'm out there arguing with him, too.

"Step aside, youngster, before you get hurt."

He's a muscle guy, with a red heart tattoo on his bare arm. There's a blue scarf tied around the other arm, and he's wearing a black leather vest. No shirt. Silver and gold chains rest on his hairy chest.

"You're not gonna steal our car," I tell him with the strongest voice I can.

The man chuckles, swinging his hair out of his eyes. So I lunge at him. He pushes me down. But I scramble up, ready to go at him again.

"You better call off your boy, toots," he says to Mama, as he pulls some chains from the back of his truck.

She grabs my arm, and I look at her, wondering why she's not calling the police or somebody to come stop this jerk.

"He's taking the car because I can't pay for it anymore," she says, pulling me out of the man's way.

I watch him back the truck to the front of our car. *My '61 Rambler Classic in pale yellow with the convertible top.* He hitches it up and then leans over the front seat of his truck. He comes over with some papers.

"Just sign these and I'll be going."

Mama does. He grunts at me from behind his sunglasses.

"See ya round, kid."

Mama and me stand there, alone, in the middle of the parking lot, watching our car roll away.

"Is God punishing us, Mama? Is that why all this is happening? Does he hate colored people, like the kids at Haley say?"

I'm standing so close to her I feel her tense up.

"Why you believe those ignorant, backwoods children who go around spouting their parents' hate, I'll never know." She squints up at me and covers her eyes from the sun. "God got nothing to do with hate, Mark. People hate, not God. Their father is the Devil, and they do the works of their father."

She leaves me and walks back to the building. I stay put and let the sun bake my brains out. I don't know much about what the Bible says, but I know Mama believes it.

So if God isn't their father, whose father is he?

6

On Monday, it happens. What I've been dreading. I see Eddie in the hall. He's talking to some boys I don't know. One of them has a couple of big combs in his hand, showing the others. I try to walk by without getting noticed, but that's like asking a mouse to walk past a room full of cats.

As I pass, one of them grabs my arm.

"Hey, white boy, what you doing up in here?"

Eddie's brows smash together, but he doesn't say a word.

I yank free. "I go here. What are *you* doing here?"

The other boys laugh. Eddie walks away.

They chide me as I go on about my business. I figured I wouldn't get anywhere with Eddie, and I was right. This is going to be a long month. Good thing it's temporary.

The bell rings, and I head to Miss Alice May's class. Compared to my other subjects, I guess I like hers the best—not because I like science all that much, but because she runs her classroom like a baseball team. It didn't take me long to notice. She decides everyone's position: who erases the board, who sweeps up after class, and who helps her collect homework.

At first, I see the same kids do the same things all the time until a

new week comes around, and they rotate. I get on her team, too. My
responsibility is erasing the board, and it's on that first assignment that
I come to class and see something I'm not expecting:

WHITE BOY GO HOME

The letters are in thick, white chalk and large enough to cover the
entire board.

I look around the room, into their faces. Their eyes give away their
guilt. One kid bursts into laughter until the girl next door hits him.

Miss Alice May is late, so I pick up the eraser to make the words
disappear, wishing I could do the same.

"Leave it."

Miss Alice May walks in, and the rustling in the room lets me know
what's going on behind me.

"Sit down, Mark."

I leave the eraser on the rail and take my seat. The room is so quiet
you could hear death. She sits on the edge of her desk and crosses her
arms. I get anxious, waiting for her to show these kids she's not taking
their mess. Maybe I'll get to see a spanking. I heard they still do that in
colored schools no matter how old you are.

"Who is responsible for this?" she asks, in a seriously teacher tone.

No one says a word, and I try to guess who in the class doesn't like
me. Is it all of them? Just a few of them? If I was at Haley—where
everyone looks like me—this stuff would never happen, well, not
about race anyway. I recall what Winston once wrote on the board
about Paul McDonald. It was funny, but it was wrong, too. When Paul
came into the room and saw PISSY PAUL PEES HIS PANTS, I could
see Paul's whole body melt like the wicked witch in the Wizard of Oz.
But all Winston got was a scolding and a warning not to do it again. I
don't know what Miss Alice May intends to do, but after being in her
class for a while, I know it's not going to stop at a warning.

"If no one is going to tell the truth, I'll have to punish all of you."

The kids fuss and complain, and one finally says, "It was Teeter. He
did it."

Everyone looks at the tattletaler in shock. Some with disgust. And I can
see how tight-knit this family is when one of their own becomes a snitch.

So it was sweaty boy. They call him Teeter? I wonder why.

"All right then. Mister Parker, come up here."

The boy Teeter pushes off from behind his wooden desk with defiance in his eyes. Everyone else murmurs about the coming judgment, like they know what it is.

Miss Alice May grabs his shoulders and leads him to the blackboard. "Tell me, Mister Parker. Does it make you a big man to make others feel small?"

"No, ma'am."

"Oh, then I guess you just get a kick out of showing how ignorant you are?"

Uproarious laughter fills the room until Miss Alice May puts up her hand. "I want you to tell the class what I expect of my students, Mister Parker, and that includes you."

Teeter seems hesitant. He doesn't turn to face us right away.

"Mister Parker, the class creed, please."

Finally, he takes a deep breath and lets it out, like it's going to take all the strength he has to follow her instructions: "No one is inferior in Miss Alice May's class, and as a colored person, I should know better. Color has held our race down for hundreds of years, but that does not give me the right to hold down others..."

I look around the room and notice some of the kids mouthing the same words Teeter is reciting at the front of the class.

"...If I am to overcome, as Reverend King tells me, I cannot show the same hatred, ignorance, and injustice that my white brothers display toward me. I'm smarter than that. I'm stronger than that, and I'm above that."

Teeter looks at Miss Alice May, and she nods.

"Thank you, Mister Parker. You may be seated."

He passes my desk on the way, but his eyes avoid me. How does he feel, having to say such things in front of a white boy? Then I catch myself. I'm not a white boy. So the words he put on the board don't apply to me. I sit a little taller in my chair and shake off the hurt I'd been feeling. This punishment is not what I expected, but somehow it fits. Like Miss Alice May's words, I know I have to be smarter, stronger, and above it all, too. Then I wonder if Philip knows about Miss Alice May's class creed.

At the bell, everyone scrambles into the hall, but Miss Alice May asks me to stay behind. She sits me down in the first desk.

"Mark, remember what happens to a caterpillar when it comes out of the cocoon?"

This seems like a pretty dumb question, but she's a science teacher, so I figure it's leading up to something. "Yes, ma'am. It turns into a butterfly."

"And do you think being a butterfly is harder than being a caterpillar?"

"I don't know. The butterfly is much better looking, and it can fly instead of crawl."

Miss Alice May smiles, but she isn't finished.

"When the butterfly is a caterpillar and creates the cocoon, it is very vulnerable. I mean, it's not safe. The bad weather could blow it away, or predators could come along and eat it. It's in constant danger."

"OK," I say, still not sure where this is going.

"Would you say the caterpillar has a lot to overcome in order to turn into a butterfly?"

"Yes, I guess so."

Miss Alice May leans in a little closer. "You Mark, are a butterfly in reverse."

"Ma'am?"

She smiles again.

"Everyone, at one time or another, has to face predators and the feeling of being unsafe. Storms come along; we all have to weather them. In your case, your storms came after instead of before. Right now you may feel like a caterpillar instead of the butterfly you felt you were before. But no matter when your adversity comes, Mark, you have to be strong and get past it."

She puts her hand on my shoulder.

"You're still a butterfly, Mark. Just because others see you as a caterpillar doesn't mean you have to believe them."

Then she walks me to the door.

"Now go out there and spread those wings, you hear me?"

———

In history, we have a substitute. I nod my way through that class until it's time for gym. Teeter is in here, too. Some of the kids say he's got it in for me after Miss Alice May made him recite the class creed, so I tighten my fists. Open, close, open, close. I need to be ready in case I get jumped.

Our gym teacher, Mr. Gaines, reminds me of the Mexicans on the farm—the migrant workers who came for a season and went home again. He has a thick mustache and biceps to match. He's a bodybuilder and won a few competitions up north. He must have a ton of blue shirts. He wears one every day. Today he has us file out onto the patchy grass. Teeter and a few other kids are eyeballing me.

"I need nine players over here," Mr. Gaines says, "and nine there."

Can it be? Are we playing baseball?

My confidence soars. This is *my* game, and my gut tells me I have to show them I can do something they can't.

"Mr. Gaines?" I interrupt. "I play in the local Babe Ruth league."

That's when Teeter and his friends make a fuss.

"No fair," one of them says. "He shouldn't even be playing."

Mr. Gaines doesn't listen. He puts me at shortstop—one of the hardest positions in baseball. *My* position.

"Can any of you pitch?" Mr. Gaines asks.

I pray Teeter raises his hand, but he doesn't. I want to knock his balls clear to Kingdom Come. Since Eddie's not in my gym class—or speaking to me for that matter—there's no way I can team up with him to teach these losers a lesson. I'm really starting to miss my old friend.

Mr. Gaines finds a kid to pitch, and the game gets underway.

"Strike one," the kid keeping score yells out. He definitely doesn't play baseball. Everybody knows only the umpire calls strikes. One of the boys who made fun of me on the basketball court is up at bat.

"Strike two."

I lock in on my position, hold my glove, and wait. "Please, please, please hit the ball over here." I pray.

WHACK

He runs fast as lightning to first base. But the boy on first isn't paying any attention and doesn't even see the ball fly over his head. That disappoints me, especially since Teeter is next at bat. We've got to get him out and stop the kid on first from scoring. It's a tall order for these clowns, but I do what I can to keep my hopes up.

"When you snooze, you lose," Teeter teases the first baseman. He stands on the mound swinging the bat around. He nearly hits the catcher.

"Ball one," the scorekeeper kid screams.

I just shake my head. What a pathetic excuse for a team.

"That wasn't a ball," I yell to Mr. Gaines, but he ignores me.

Teeter scoots his behind back like he's Jackie Robinson or somebody, grinning from ear to ear. That makes me even more determined to knock his block off if that ball of his comes my way. I also found out how he got his name: he fell off a teeter-totter as a kid and broke his nose. Now it kinda teeters to one side. That bit of news makes me smile all over again as I wait for him to slip up and strike out.

WHACK

Teeter surprises me with the strength of his hit, and the ball heads straight for second base. But these kids have no skills. It soars right past the second baseman and plops onto the ground. I scurry to scoop it up, run to second, and smash my right foot on the bag.

OUT

But I'm not through yet. I quickly turn to first, prepare my arm for the hardest throw I can muster, and then let her rip. To my surprise, the first baseman is ready and can actually catch. Then *whammo*, Teeter is out, too.

I reconsider what I said about the guy on first. After that performance, he can play on my team any day. It's the sweetest double play ever. I even earn some woof tickets I can use for later (that's Douglass slang for bragging rights).

"Great job, Lawson," Mr. Gaines says. "I'll have to come out and see you play sometime."

It's nice to hear him say that, but I don't believe he'll ever do it. Most coloreds stay away from the ball games due to all the insults thrown at the colored players. If colored folks do come, they have to sit in the separate area where Eddie's father sits. Change is coming, but not that fast. That's when it dawns on me: If I ever went to another team's game, where would they make me sit?

————

It takes me a minute to get used to the new me, and just when I'm getting better at it, something sets me back. Like the stuff we're learning in history. I know Mr. Jordan can't avoid the subject of slavery. That's what we're studying. But today, mulattos come up. Not a subject I want to hear about or talk about. I wish I could leave while he explains how slave masters took female slaves and got them pregnant. It's cruel and makes me sick to my stomach. After class I tell him how I feel.

"It's not that I don't want to learn about mulattos and folks like that, it's...well. It makes kids stare at me, sort of like I'm, you know, strange."

As soon as I say that, I know it sounds stupid, but I can't really explain it any other way. I wish I could just make the whole room the same color.

"It's a fact, Mark, and I'm obliged to teach the facts." Mr. Jordan explains. "The origin of the black mulatto is something you need to know in order to understand the double standard slave owners had regarding race mixing. What would you have me do, son? Ignore the facts so that you can feel better about yourself? Isn't that what the slave masters tried to do?"

"But I just don't like hearing about it."

"How much did you know about slavery or mulattos before you came to Douglass?"

"Well, I knew some mulattos on the farm in Greensboro, but I didn't really know anything about them. They didn't teach a lot about slavery at my other schools—just the cotton gin, how slaves were counted for voting, and how the North took advantage of us to win the war. Stuff like that."

"I see."

That's when he decides to make us all do a written report on mulattos.

I haven't set foot in the Montgomery Public Library since Mama got fired. I'm still mad at them, but I don't have a choice since this is the only library in town. I take a seat at one of the round tables at the end of a tall bookcase and pull out my notebook. I'm not sure where to start, so I ask the librarian lady stacking books on the shelf behind me.

"Excuse me," I say, waiting for her to turn around. "Can you help me find out something about mulattos?"

I guess I say it too loud. Two people, sitting at a table nearby, look up. One is white, the other black.

"That depends, young man," says the librarian. "what are you trying to find out?'

"Their history, I guess, and why people treat them as Black."

The librarian's face turns red, and her lips purse. She turns back to stacking her books and says, "I don't think I can help you there, but you'll find some references in the card catalog."

The ends of my eyebrows move together. I think she's brushing me off, but I'm not sure, so I just say thank you and head to the card catalog. I stand there looking up and down the wooden dresser filled with little drawers. Each has a small window with letters and numbers on it. From that, you're supposed to be able to find what you want, but I can't understand any of it. I scratch my head and look around. Maybe another librarian might be more helpful. The room is large, with a few people sitting here and there at tables, reading or writing things down. I don't see another librarian, so I head to the front desk.

"Psst," says a voice. I look back and see it's one of the two people sitting at the table near mine. The black person.

He waves me over, and I go.

"Hi," he says, "I'm Ken." Then he turns to the other guy. "This is Jack."

"I'm Mark."

"We're students at the university. Do you want to sit with us? Maybe we can help you find what you're looking for."

"That would be great," I say. "Let me get my stuff."

I go back to my table, and as I gather up my things, the librarian watches me. When our eyes meet, she huffs and goes back to her shelving. I shrug and move to the other table.

"I heard you say you're researching mulattos," the white one, Jack, says. "Is this a school project or something?'

"Yes, for history. I mean, black history."

They smile at each other.

"So what is it you need to know?" asks Ken, the black one.

As I look at the two of them, I wonder if I should tell them I'm mulatto. I mean, colored. Black. All the different words are so confusing. But these two don't look like they'd have a problem with whatever I am. They're dressed in jeans and short-sleeved knit shirts. The white guy has shoulder-length hair, like he's in a band. The black one has short, thick hair. I go ahead and talk to them about it.

"Well, I..."

All of a sudden my lips tighten, and I can't get out what I want to say.

"It's cool, man. Just spill it," says Jack. He seems pretty cool himself.

"I guess I'm...mulatto. At least that's what I'm told. But this really *is* a school project." I add quickly, just so they know I wasn't lying.

They just nod and don't drag it out of me.

"So, you came to research mulattos?" asks Ken.

I scoot closer to the table and rest my elbows.

"I guess I came to find out why the slave masters didn't raise the kids they had with slaves. I mean, since they were half white."

I really want the answer to this question since I didn't get to ask it in class.

"Yeah, that was a downer," says Jack. "You'd think they'd claim the white-looking ones."

Ken acts like he can't believe Jack said that.

"But my teacher says they tried to blame those kids on the other slaves. I mean, the men."

"Your teacher's right," says Ken. "But when mulatto children started popping up on plantations all over the South, it was obvious where they came from since male slaves had literally no access to white women."

"Really," I say. "That makes sense."

"The whole issue of mulattos and their human rights was very complicated," says Ken. "Let's go find some information, and we can discover some of the answers together."

Ken gets up, and we go back to the card catalog. He's a whiz at using it, and soon we have lots of material on our table. He points to information we got off something called microfilm. It's old US Census records.

"It says here that in 1850, the census takers started counting free coloreds—usually mulattos—separate from whites and blacks. But this caused a lot of problems. Those who supported slavery didn't want freemen counted because it meant they were actually people." Ken's face shows disappointment.

"Yeah," says Jack. "That would mean they had rights and should be allowed to vote."

"I remember learning that slaves could be counted as three-quarters of a vote for slave owners," I say.

"Right," says Ken. "If they claimed the kids, they couldn't count them as slaves, and they'd have to give them the same rights white people enjoyed. Allowing mulattos to be counted separately from slaves could cause some political problems."

"And look at this." Ken points to the Xerox copies. "By the 1890 census, they used a really crazy system for counting colored people. They broke it down into four types: blacks, mulattos, quadroons, and octoroons."

"And they didn't even tell the census takers how to determine which was which," says Jack.

Ken keeps reading. "Says here, the word 'black' should be used to describe those persons who have three-fourths or more black blood; 'mulatto,' those persons who have from three-eighths to five-eighths black blood; 'quadroon,' those persons who have one-fourth black blood; and 'octoroon,' those persons who have one-eighth or any trace of black blood."

"Heavy," says Jack.

Ken nods and leans closer to me.

"So Mark, you say your mom is white and your dad was mulatto?

So if your old man looked like you, you'd probably fall into the octoroon category."

"Yeah," says Jack. "Like, you're not really black at all, man. You're, like, passing for Black."

'Passing for Black' was a new term for me. I'd never heard anyone say that before.

"But then there's that 'one drop' rule," says Jack. "The one that says you're black no matter how much white blood your folks gave you."

"I learned that in school, too," I say. "It seemed kind of dumb to me."

"It is dumb," says Ken, "but I don't think some people will ever accept that, even with all the progress that's being made in the struggle."

"Struggle?" I ask.

"The movement, man, the struggle for civil rights. Ken and I do some volunteer work for Snick," says Jack.

"Who?"

"The Student Nonviolent Coordinating Committee. We're the ones who helped integrate this library."

"Wow," I say, thinking it's cool that they're working together. Black and white.

"Yeah, and we're not done yet. We've got to help kids like yourself learn more about the past so you can make the right decisions about your future."

Ken agrees.

I glance over at the librarian. We're talking low, but I bet she can hear our conversation. If she does, she's not saying anything.

"So, Mark, the bottom line on this mulatto thing is, it doesn't matter what they call you; it's what you think about yourself in here." Ken taps his chest.

"And don't let it mess up your head," says Jack. "Since you have both races in your blood, you have to stand up for both."

Ken nods at Jack.

"Thanks, guys. I'm sure I've got enough to write my paper now."

Ken holds out his palm, and at first I'm not sure what he wants, then Jack slides his palm across Ken's. Ken holds it out to me again. I slide mine against his so I can give him some skin, too.

"All right," they say, nodding.

———

When I get home, I pull out my paper and think. I start to see that race is just an idea made up by people who want to control other people and make them feel less important or less powerful. That must be what Mama meant when she said this country wants you to believe you're 'less than.'

Ken and Jack say that in some European countries, there's no such thing as passing for white or any of those names we found for black people. I guess Melissa's at school being white and passing for black with her colored friends—I mean, her black friends. Ken says black people today don't want to be called colored or Negro. "Black" is a word they chose for themselves. It makes them feel proud of their African roots.

When I look at my hands, I see white skin, even though people call me colored. I found out that the word "colored" was used first for mulattos, and then they started calling all blacks "colored." I never thought that word made sense, and now that I know where it comes from, it makes even less sense.

Why does it have to be so complicated? I just want to do like Jack says. I want to be proud of both sides of my family.

7

Montgomery doesn't really have seasons. I mean, it doesn't go from winter to spring to summer to fall like the pictures we used to draw in grade school. It's pretty much warm all the time, and today it's hickory hot.

Now that school is out for the summer, I'm back to walking around town visiting every business I can to see if they might have something for a teenager to do.

I catch the bus downtown and head to Lawrence Avenue. I plan to stop in at Alexa Drug Company. They sell all kinds of things: prescriptions, candy, and cigarettes. Just about anything a person could want. It sits next to Tara Pawn Brokers, which is the one place Mama told me not to go. She says the wrong kind of people hang out in pawnshops.

I walk up to the storefront window so I can peek inside to see what kind of work they do in a drugstore. I have to make sure I know what to say when I finally go in. A few customers mill around in front of an eyeglasses display. A woman is in one aisle marked COLD MEDICINE. I guess she's trying to decide what to buy. There's a man in a white coat. Must be the druggist.

I pace in front of the window trying to decide whether to go in.

"What you doing out here?"

It's Ray, and I'm surprised to see him. I'm also surprised he's talking to me. We haven't said too much to each other since the day I came back to practice. But since then he's loosened up on the field, and I'm hoping he can get over my race long enough for us to beat Bixal. He's also not dressed like he's been working, which he usually does on Saturdays.

"I'm looking for a job," I tell him.

Ray looks around me to see inside the store. He cocks his head.

"You don't wanna work in there. Old man Saunders is as crooked as a dog's hind leg. Besides, he don't hire kids."

That bit of news knocks the wind out of my sails.

"Well, I wasn't sure I wanted to work in a store anyway."

"If you really want to work, you ought to go over to Bush Construction. They got an opening for a part-timer. He don't mind if you're colored either, since y'all like to work hard."

He raises an eyebrow, but I don't bite. If Ray is trying to get me riled, it won't work. I'm more interested in what he's saying, not how he's saying it. I stick to the subject.

"But that's where you and Hank work, and I thought Mr. Bush only took two at a time?"

"Where I used to work. I'm not there anymore."

"Why, what happened?"

"Well, I guess you'll find out sooner or later. My parents bought a house in Autauga County, so we're moving. I'll be going to a private school up there. The house is real nice, too. It's got a pool..."

After Ray says the word "moving," my brain shuts down. I can't hear anything else he says. Moving means our chance to beat Bixal is as good as gone. Gone to Autauga County to a private school.

"You can't move," I say. "Not now. I mean. Are you moving *now*?"

My heart races, hoping he tells me he'll be around until after the state championship.

"My dad's getting a transfer, and my mom don't work. She's already up there decorating the place. Pop and me are packing up the easy stuff this weekend before the movers come. We'll be gone by the end of next week."

"But what about the game? What about our triple threat against Bixal? Can't you come back to play? We can't do it without you."

I hope I'm getting through to him, but his smile tells me something else. He rubs his finger under his nose and says, "Well, I guess you two niggers are gonna have to figure that out on your own."

Then he smirks and walks away. Just like that.

I don't know what it's like to be electrocuted, but it can't feel any worse than what's shaking my whole body right now, watching him go. Anger and hatred well up in my heart, but there's nothing I can do about it. I taste tears in the corners of my mouth.

"Hatred is a disease," my Pa used to say. "A stinking, festering disease that eats up everything inside you until there's nothing left worth keeping."

Pa was right, and although I hate Ray as strong as anyone could hate anything right now, I turn the other way and head home, hoping my insides end up with something worth keeping.

———

Ray doesn't show up for practice this week either, and I'm glad. I don't know what I might do if I had to see him again. From the expression on Billy's face, he knows about Ray. When I get to the bench, he's talking about it.

"Yeah, he told me last week," Billy tells Hank. While he talks, his head is down. He just keeps kicking the dust with the toe of his sneaker.

"We'd been friends since kindergarten. Played peewee together, too… and other things." Billy looks up like he just noticed me. He doesn't have to mention those 'other things.' I know what the three of them used to do at Alabama State.

"Now he's gone, and it's your fault," he says, pointing at me. "You niggers ran him off, trying to go to school with us."

I step back in case he tries to slug me. Instead, he spits on the ground, right in front of my feet.

Hank sneers at me too before they both walk over to Coach Collier, who's trying to figure out what we're gonna do without Ray. I wait a few moments before I follow. I don't want to share the same air with them.

Now that we're short a first baseman, Coach Collier is going to have a tough time finding a replacement who will be as good in that spot as Ray—it's the only thing Ray did that deserved the word "good" in front of it.

"Being that it's this late in the season, we might have to forfeit," says Billy.

"Forfeit?" says Coach Collier, angrier about it than I am. "We ain't gonna forfeit. We're gonna get somebody on this team to play first. We got three alternates on our bench, and one of them has to get us into that game."

Coach sure is taking this hard. As for Billy, all he cares about is Ray leaving.

"Of the three alternates, two can play second and third, and the other one is pretty good in the outfield," says Coach Collier, talking out loud like we don't know this already. But we understand. He needs to hear himself figure it out. "We know we can count on Mark to hold down the shortstop position, so let's take Peter out of right field and put him on first, then let one of the alternates play his position."

Peter smirks like he knew this day would come. He's a great player, but his cockiness makes me afraid for him.

"No," says Billy.

Right away I know what he's thinking. With Peter on first, it means our triple threat is turning into a real threat. That's because all three of us—me, Eddie, and Peter—are colored.

"It's not your decision," Coach says to Billy, who's clearly not happy. "We got a game to win. Now either you get with the program, or we'll find a place for you off the field."

"Don't you talk to my boy like that, Collier. He's got a right to his opinion," says Coach Justice, tobacco stuffed in his cheek.

"Yes, he does, as long as that's all it is." Coach Collier spits back. "Whether you like it or not, Justice, this team is integrated, and I'm going to use the best players I've got, no matter what color they are. If you have a problem with that, I suggest you take it up with league officials."

Me and the guys sit there in silence. We never hear Coach Collier talk that way to Coach Justice, and it makes me feel proud. He stood up for the team, the *whole* team.

After practice, Billy and Coach Justice leave right away. Billy was worse than usual today, so I ask Coach Collier if he knows what's going on.

"Come here, son." He puts his arm around my shoulder. "You remember Billy's older brother Matt?"

"Yeah."

"Well, he got called up by the Army. They sent him to Vietnam."

Vietnam is bad news; I know that much. That war's been going on since I was three years old, and lots of kids have lost brothers, uncles, cousins, and dads to it. Billy really looks up to Matt, so I can see why he's upset since he's also losing his best friend. I reconsider trying to get my Mantle back. It always made me feel better. Maybe it'll help him, too.

Over by the bench, I hear some of the guys talking about Ray's family moving out of the county. I stand as far away as I can but close enough to hear.

"Lots of kids will be gone next year," says Hank. "It's the only way to avoid integration. My pop says the courts can't force schools outside the county to integrate. He says we might be moving next year, too."

"There's some new segregated academies springing up on the outskirts of town," says Winston, "but my parents don't want to leave Montgomery, so I guess I'll be here when schools integrate all the way."

The other guys razz him and muss his hair.

"You're gonna be a nigger lover, huh, Winston?"

He swats at their hands.

"No, I'm just not that worried about going to school with them, that's all. We play ball with them, so school can't be that bad."

"Not until they start dating your sister and taking your lunch money. Then you'll change your mind," says Hank.

"Ah, you guys." Winston turns to leave. His eyes meet mine. "You hear that, Lawson? I ain't afraid of your kind. You tell that King fella I said so."

The guys laugh, and Winston beams. Seems like he's happy they're happy.

I know he isn't as bad as the others, but when you're around a bunch of kids who want to egg you on, sometimes you have to say things to impress them. That way they don't think you're a yella belly. Winston is one of those kids. Good thing Peter didn't hear him.

Before I leave the field, I see Eddie and Peter talking next to the batting cage, so I go over to join them.

"Welcome to the triple threat," I say to Peter, offering a handshake. He looks at me and then gets right back to their conversation, as if I'm not there:

"I told you I wasn't gonna make it to practice on account of my trip to Mississippi," Peter explains to Eddie. "My brother kept bugging me about going to a rally to see Stokely Carmichael."

"You mean that young guy that's been hanging around with Dr. King?"

"Yeah, I guess. Anyway, I thought I was gonna be bored to death, but the guy had some cool things to say. Matter of fact, he said something I'm gonna start using: "Black Power.""

I know I'm looking stupid standing here with my head going back and forth between Eddie and Peter, but I'm hearing stuff I don't know a thing about, so I'm trying to get in on the conversation. "Who's Stokely Carmichael?"

Eddie turns his head slightly but doesn't look right at me, like he's throwing crumbs off the side of their conversation. "He's a student who fights for civil rights, like Dr. King—"

"Oh, you best believe he's more than that *now*," says Peter. "He's talking radical, like revolution-type stuff. He don't want to get no more beatings; that's what he said. You know he been arrested 27 times?"

"Nuh uh," Eddie says.

"Yeah, and he told the crowd down there that he ain't asking no whiteys for freedom no more, he's gonna get his with black power."

Eddie's eyebrow rises like he's not sure he should believe Peter, but he never says he doesn't. "If that Mr. Carmichael keeps on," says Eddie, "he's gonna mess up everything Dr. King worked so hard to get us—"

"Get us? What did he get us, Eddie? Besides whooped upside the head? For all I care, King can take his kowtowing attitude somewhere else, 'cause we don't need no Uncle Tom leading us."

If thoughts were kindling wood, Eddie'd be a bonfire. From the look in his eyes, Peter's radical talk ain't goin' down so well. When Peter gets on his high horse, it gives me the creeps, so I just walk away.

"Hey, hey Lawson, where you going?" Peter calls to me, so I stop and turn around, knowing that I'm probably making a big mistake listening to anything he has to say. "I hear your mama's white, but your daddy was a redbone." Peter snickers. He looks to Eddie for support, but Eddie's expression doesn't change. He just stands there, stone-faced.

"Aw man, you know I'm just kidding around with the boy." Peter doesn't take his eyes off me. He comes closer. Close enough to feel his breath on my face. He's taller than me and bigger. "I'm sure he's hip to why white women want black men," Peter says as Eddie joins us. Then Peter smiles wide in my face. "You know what they say, once you go Black, you never go back—"

Without warning, Eddie pushes Peter, and fists fly, so I jump in, too. I've wanted to fight somebody all week. I hop on Peter's back and wrap my arms tight around his neck while Eddie lands blows to his stomach.

Soon Hank and Boz rush in, and we all get to fighting. By the time it's all over, we're filthy, tired, and bloody. Peter lost a front tooth, Bosley's neck is full of scratches, and I'm missing some of my hair. Coach penalizes all of us one game, and of course we lose, but to me it's worth it. I haven't felt this good in a long time.

8

———————

On the day of the state championship, we're headed to Greensboro, and I'm nervous as an ant at an aardvark convention. Eddie and I still aren't talking even though he stood up for me against Peter. When I asked him about it at the next practice, he kept swinging his bat, ignoring me. Maybe he wasn't helping me at all. Maybe he fought Peter over Dr. King. At least Bosley still speaks to me, but not around Billy or Hank, which means he's really not speaking to me at all.

As far as Peter is concerned, I hear he's a delinquent. Philip says it's all over the grapevine that Peter spends most of his time skipping school to sell marijuana for his big brother. If Coach knew about that, Peter'd be off the team. So if he makes us lose this game, I'm sure gonna tell it.

On the ride up, none of the guys sit next to me as they pile onto the bus. I watch each of them, their eyes searching for a spot. Bosley is coming behind Winston, so I figure he'll be my seatmate. When Winston gets close to me, his eyes meet mine. He always sits near the front, but now he's right next to my seat. He jerks his head, which tells me to get over by the window. I scoot as close to it as I can, and he sits.

We don't talk. Just ride. So I look out the window to see if I can recognize any parts of Greensboro that I used to know.

All the guys rode up on the team bus, except Eddie and Peter. Eddie came with his father, and I guess Peter's gonna get there somehow. He'd better.

When we get to the field and unload, I see Eddie. He's talking to his father, who is standing on the other side of the chain-link fence. There's an opening near him for fans to come onto the field, but he doesn't. Guess he's not going to sit in the colored section either.

The field stretches for miles, and the grass is greener than a four-leaf clover. Being in my old hometown starts to bring back memories. Mama let me come on the bus since we don't have a car, but she really wanted to bring me. I'm glad she couldn't. I don't think it would have been good for her. The doctor says she needs to rest as much as possible.

My eyes scour the stands just in case I see any familiar faces. I'm really searching for Johnny Mack. I've been hoping all week he might be here.

All over the field the lights sit high up on tall wood poles in case it gets dark during the game. Since our team plays first, we don't have to worry about that. Fences block off different parts of the field. Our section is the biggest. There's a building with a green roof where the bathrooms are located and a concession stand to the left of us. Best of all, we've got a real live dugout, and I can't wait to take my seat on the benches below.

"Nervous?" asks Coach Collier as we unload the bus.

"Yeah, who wouldn't be? This is the most important game of my whole life."

He smiles and hands me the bag of bats. He takes the balls, and we go to our dugout. "You just do your best, son; the rest will take care of itself."

I nod, though I'm not as confident as he is. Guess that's why he's the coach.

We have a little time, so I walk over to the stands. As I go, I look up, trying to see the people. The seats rise seven or eight rows. Lots of fathers and sons. Women with babies and kids running up and down the stairs. A man selling peanuts walks among them, but most people are lined up at the concession stand to get their hot dogs and drinks before the game starts.

Just at the end of the fifth row I see—I mean, I think I see him. "Hey Johnny," I call. "Johnny Mack."

He turns, and at first he doesn't seem to recognize me. Then his hands go up, and he steps over some people until he gets to the stairs. When he comes down, I meet him on the first row.

"Hey, Mark. How you doing?"

"I'm fine. Fine. How about you?"

"Great."

"Your mom and dad?"

"They're fine, too." Johnny points them out.

I put my hand above my eyes to block the sun. They wave, though I doubt they know who they're waving at, and I can't make out their faces.

"So what brings you to the game?" I ask him.

"My little brother's playing later on. He's pretty good, too."

"Your brother? Not that scrawny kid we used to chase into the barn?"

We laugh.

"Yep, that's the one. The little league tournaments are held here, too."

"Cool," I say, smiling so hard it hurts.

"It sure is good to see you. You still trying to dance?"

Boy, does that bring back memories. I kicked up a little dust back then, meaning I could do a little something. Back then Johnny said I had rhythm for a white boy, and I took that as a compliment. Those colored kids on the farm could cut a rug, as my Pa used to say.

Right then it dawns on me: Johnny Mack doesn't know I'm colored, and since he's colored, why is he sitting in the white section?

"What's wrong?" he asks. That's when I know it's showing on my face. I'm not sure what to say, but since I might not see him again, I tell the truth.

"Johnny, I'm not white. I mean, I found out that I'm...colored. Like you."

Johnny's head backs away from mine. His eyes narrow. He's silent.

"So-o-o, what are you doing sitting over here?" I ask, looking around like it must be a joke or something. "I mean, won't they make you move?"

Johnny turns his back on me and heads back up the stairs. He never even says goodbye. I watch him go back to his family. When he gets there, they all sit down with their popcorn and hot dogs. They never even look my way.

When I turned in my mulatto paper to Mr. Jordan a few weeks ago, he told me that when colored people decide to pass, they have to leave everything behind—including family and friends. It's the only way they can do it without being exposed. I'm still standing there when Coach Collier comes to get me.

"We're about ready, son."

I go with him, but my mind's not on the game. It's on the fact that I just lost somebody I thought was a good friend. Somebody who's decided to be someone else.

Coach counts off. "Winston, Bosley, Hank...but where's Peter?" He looks around the field. "If he doesn't show up, we'll have to put in one of the alternates."

That's the last thing I want to hear. We'll lose for sure.

"Coach, I'm worried about Peter," says Billy, practically out of breath. "I've looked all over this field for him, and he's not here."

Coach puts his hand up. "I know, I know." He looks at his watch. "We'll give him a few more minutes before we pull in a replacement. I've got up to fifteen minutes before the game to make a roster change."

Eddie is headed toward the mound.

"Go out there and warm up with him," Coach Collier tells us.

As we go out to join Eddie, the catcalls and cursing begin. Just like at home.

I see Eddie's dad watching the people in the stands. His fingers cling to the links in the fence. He doesn't respond to the insults, and it reminds me of the maid at Billy's house. I guess it's what those civil rights people teach them. That peaceable stuff Eddie talks about.

"Coach Collier." An umpire comes to our dugout. "Is your roster set?"

Coach looks around again, holding up the brim of his cap.

Then all of a sudden here comes Peter, rounding the corner like his life depends on it. And to me, it does. I let out a sigh of relief.

"Sorry I'm late, Coach. My brother had something to do."

I look over by the parked cars and see the one Peter jumped out of. Two rough-looking black men stand outside by the door of a Cutlass. Nice car. And that paint job wasn't cheap.

"That's my brother and his friend," Peter says from over my shoulder. "If anything goes down, they'll protect me."

I turn my head toward him but don't say a word. He goes to the bench, and I keep my eye on the two men. They both have on leather jackets even though it's hot out here. Dark sunglasses. Black combs rest in their hair.

We all stand for the national anthem and cover our hearts with our caps. Peter refuses to do it, and the crowd boos. Eddie is standing to his right, and Billy's on his left.

"If you know what's good for you, you'll do it," Billy whispers to Peter.

"I don't owe these peckerwoods nothin'," Peter responds, and I can tell Billy's got it in for him.

By the bottom of the sixth, we're playing well despite the name-calling. It never lets up. Eddie's arm is on fire, and I'm glad the crowd isn't getting to him. Every once in a while I look over at his dad. He's still there. Watching. Peter's brother and his friend are standing there now, too. One has his hand inside his jacket. It stays there the whole game.

The tension between Billy and Peter is getting worse, and Coach has had to talk to them several times.

"You throw this game for us, Peter, and you're history," Billy warns him, but Peter just waves him off. He's doing a better job at first base than I expected, and I'm praying nothing goes wrong.

Coming into the seventh inning, the score is two to one in our favor. The Bloodhounds' game is getting intense, but we have to hang on.

The batter is up. Runners are on first and second. Eddie throws the pitch. It's a hard grounder. Eddie scoops it up and throws it toward second, where I catch it and get our first out. Then I immediately throw to Peter, who gets the batter out.

Yes!

But something strange happens. The runner headed for third, slips, and falls face down in the dirt. He tries to make it to the base, but Peter immediately throws to third, and Bosley gets him out.

A triple play! I can't believe it! We won! We really won!

We all run into the dugout cheering, patting Peter on the head, and slapping his backside.

There's anger in the stands. People are coming onto the field. They're headed for our dugout. Paper cups are thrown on the grass, and fights are breaking out between white and colored fans.

Peter's brother and his friend come through the fence opening and start busting heads with something that looks like a nightstick.

"Run to the bus," Coach yells, trying to round us all up.

I don't see Eddie anywhere. His father isn't at the fence. I hope they get away.

People are running in every direction, and the police pull up. Instead of coming with us, Peter runs toward the brawl. He's joining in.

Is he crazy?

"I said get to the bus." Coach pushes me away and then heads toward Peter. But the crowd is thick and pushes him around like a pinball game. White kids pick up rocks and throw them at any colored person they see. Mothers with babies run toward the exits. One colored woman loses her shoe and stumbles to the ground. She's immediately attacked. Several people are down, bleeding.

As soon as I get to the bus, someone yells, "Get them niggers."

I look in that direction to see Peter, his brother, and his friend jump into their car and peel out; two white men go after them. So do the police.

Why didn't he listen to Coach and come with us?

Not long after we get on the bus, it's shaking. Out the window I see some guys are trying to turn it over.

"Put all your weight on it," Winston yells. He pulls the door handle and shuts us in. "And stay low 'case they bust the windows."

Me, Boz, and a few other guys rush to that side of the bus, leaning against it to keep it steady. Billy's helping too, which is a shock. I'm surprised he's not out there fighting the coloreds.

When Coach returns, he shoves the men out of the way. Since he's a big guy, they don't shove back.

"If you don't get the hell away from this bus, I swear I'll call out every mother's son of you I know and get ya arrested. Now git."

"You coon lover," says one.

"Communist," yells another. But they leave.

Coach pushes against the door. When I let him in, he steps over me and grabs the wheel. His hands tremble trying to start the engine, but he manages to get us out of there.

"That's exactly what I wanted to avoid," Coach says to me as he drives. His voice shakes. He hits the steering wheel with the palm of his hand. "Stupid racism. Stupid, stupid, stupid."

I sit there in silence on the seat across from him. I used to think Coach didn't care about colored people one way or the other, but I guess I was wrong. More than that, it's about what happened out there —how all those people were so mad Peter won us the game. They wanted to hurt him just because he's colored.

A chill walks up my back.

That could've been me if they knew I was colored. They could've been coming after me.

When Coach gets us to our home field, all the kids' parents are waiting. I watch them excitedly tell their moms and dads what happened and how we won the game. I wish my Pa was here to meet me, too.

Coach Collier takes me home and comes in with me so he can explain things to Mama.

"...Mrs. Lawson, I apologize for getting your son mixed up in such a mess."

"Thank you for getting him home safely."

Coach looks at me. "I'll let you know the minute I hear from Eddie. I sure hope he's all right."

"Me, too," I say, and I really mean it.

After Coach Collier leaves, I put down my glove, pull off my cap, and go to the kitchen to get a glass of water. Mama wants one too, so I get it and bring them both into the living room. She's got her bottle of pills on the coffee table these days since she spends most of her time in here.

"I got a call from the social worker last evening," says Mama. "There was a mistake on our application for food stamps. It said three children, not one, so they cut our allowance."

I shake my head in disgust. I don't have to ask what that means. I've just got to find a job.

She takes a pill from the bottle and then asks, "Did you see any of your old friends in Greensboro?"

I know she's trying to change the subject to make me feel better, but it doesn't work. All it does is call to mind what happened between me and Johnny.

I stare at my glass before I sip. Inside, the water is cool, but outside, it sweats. I never understood that, like I'll never understand his decision.

"No, ma'am. I didn't see any of my old friends."

9

The next morning I go over to Eddie's just to see if he's OK. Even if he doesn't talk to me, at least I'll know whether he got roughed up or if he made it back at all. Mama's still asleep, so I finish up the dishes for her and pull the door closed behind me.

It's not a long walk to West Fifth from the Eastman Apartments. Matter of fact, I'm closer to Eddie's house now than I was when we lived on Boultier. As I walk, I pay more attention to how different it is on this side of Carter Hill Road, but not in the same way I used to. The houses don't seem so run-down, and the sidewalks not so broken up. It's *my* neighborhood now, and every nook and cranny's become familiar.

I'm not sure what I'll say to him if he comes to the door. He'll likely slam it on me like I did him. But for some reason it doesn't bother me. What's important is knowing he's safe and that he didn't get caught up in that mob yesterday.

I just wish he would understand that I don't hate him. That I was confused and scared. Hurt. I didn't mean to treat him like an outcast. If anyone knows how that feels, it's me.

Walking up his block, I see Mr. Goshay. He's in the backyard cutting grass with one of those push mowers. That's one thing I don't miss about the house on Boultier: those hot days cutting all that grass.

I stop in front of the house until he sees me.

"Go on inside. He's in there."

I nod and walk up the steps and onto the porch.

I knock and wait. The old rocking chair is still here, and so is that mangy cat that lives next door. He's over here more than he's at home.

The door squeak gets my attention.

"What you want?"

Eddie is shirtless in a pair of blue jeans. His hair is wild, like he just woke up.

I stick my hands in my pockets, and for a split second I wonder why *he's* not cutting the grass.

"Wanted to make sure you got home all right, but I saw your dad in the yard, so I figured you got away safe."

I look away and squint from the noonday sun.

"Yeah, the same way you did, Peter, right?"

I frown. "What're you talking about?"

Eddie pushes the screen door, so I back out of the way. He sits in the rocking chair and holds his head. "I'm talking about you and Coach Collier. Peter ain't been home yet. Who knows what's happened to him?" He looks up from the rocking chair. "Why didn't you help him?"

"Help him? As far as I could tell, he didn't *want* any help. Him and his brother, or whoever that was, seemed to be taking care of themselves."

Didn't he see Peter run into the crowd like it was Mardi Gras?

Eddie stands and gets in my face.

"And that's exactly what I'm talking about. You don't care *nothing* about colored folks, or else you woulda known that Peter was just going along. He didn't want to be *no* part of that mess—"

"And how was I supposed to know that? I'm not a mind reader and neither is Coach, last I checked—"

"This ain't funny, Mark. Peter could be in the woods somewhere, dead. If you were really colored, you'd a made sure he got on that bus."

He pushes past me and lets the screen door slam behind him.

"What do you want from me, Eddie?" I yell through the black mesh. "What?"

He doesn't respond, so I step off the porch and go my own way, no closer to making up with him than I was before I came.

How can he blame that on me or on Coach?

It's not like Coach didn't try to get to Peter, but that crowd was rowdy, and Peter didn't want to come. I decide right then and there that I'm not gonna take the blame for that one. Eddie's just being spiteful.

Peter's probably just fine, and Eddie's doing all that worrying for nothing.

———

On my way home I pass the basketball court. They don't have one on the other side of Carter Hill, at least not that I've seen. Probably got one inside Huntingdon College, but I doubt it. It's either football or baseball at most white schools. Basketball is like a third-wheel sport around here.

As I walk, I watch them play. Then I see Teeter. I still haven't forgotten what he wrote up on the board about me, but after what I've seen from the white boys on my ball team, he's no worse than they are, so I go over there to get a closer look.

"Hey Mark, come on out here so I can show you some moves."

I look around to see who else could have the name Mark before I respond.

"Yeah, you, Lawson. Come on out here."

I take my time getting to the middle of the court and stop right on the free throw line. It's fading, but you can still see it. The basket has a new net.

"So you want to learn how to play this game?" Teeter asks.

"Sure," I say. I can't make friends with Eddie, but there's no reason why I can't make friends with somebody else, and if he's not fooling around trying to embarrass me, learning this game might help my reputation.

He steps back a few paces and then bounces the ball to me. I catch it, and he claps real slow, like folks do when they're not enthusiastic. I bounce it back.

"The first thing you need to learn is how to dribble." He bends down and bounces the ball from one hand to the other. "This is dribbling."

The guys on the sidelines aren't saying anything, just watching.

"Is this on the level?"

Teeter's eyes roll. He motions for the other guys to come onto the court.

"Look, Mark, me and the guys talked about it, and we think you're an OK cat. And even though you look like a honky, we know you ain't one, so we figured we'd give you a break, cool?"

I look around at the other guys. They nod at me, and that makes me breathe easier.

"Cool."

"All right, now the first thing you gotta do is make sure you don't let nobody take the ball from you..."

I start to get the hang of it and ask lots of questions.

"This one-handed dribbling thing is pretty tricky."

"You'll get used to it," says Teeter. "Here's what I do."

As he shows me his moves, Eddie comes over to the court. He watches us but doesn't say anything.

Teeter throws the ball to me, and I shoot the basket.

"All right," says Teeter. "You made one."

As he and the other guys pat me on the back, Eddie turns to leave. But at least I found a friend in Teeter. After all that's been going on, I need a colored boy to know I'm not the enemy.

————

It took the league about a week to reorganize our award ceremony. Awards usually get handed out right after the game, but ours didn't since we had to get out of Greensboro in a hurry.

We stand on the field at Huntingdon College. Once I get hold of my trophy, I'm on cloud nine, and my smile is so wide it hurts. I've wanted this since forever. Getting that trophy makes up for just about everything that's gone wrong since I got that letter from the Board of Education. I can feel tears rolling down my cheeks when they hand it to me—winner's tears.

But something isn't right. By the time all the trophies have been handed out and we're lining up for the camera, Peter still hasn't shown up.

"All right, time for a photo with the MVP," the photographer says.

"We'll be skipping that one today," Coach says.

I look over at Eddie. My throat tightens.

At first I figure Peter just doesn't care about trophies and such, but that doesn't seem normal for a kid who plays as good as he does. When Peter doesn't show up for our next practice, I ask Coach Collier about it.

"I tried to call his house after the game, but no one answered," says Coach. "A few days later, the line was disconnected."

"What do you think happened?"

Coach Collier rubs his eyelids with the tips of his fingers. "I don't know, but I sure hope it's not what I think it is."

"What?"

"Son, you've lived in the South long enough to know what can happen to a colored boy who talks and acts like Peter. I aim to contact his high school to find out what they know, and I hope he's just gone off somewhere with his family."

Coach is right, and I could kick myself for not realizing it myself. I sigh, remembering what Eddie said at his house the other day. Coloreds face a real danger here, and it never occurred to me just how much until now.

Since that day, all kinds of rumors have been flying around about what happened to Peter: Some say he got beat up so bad that he's crippled and living up north. Others say he just decided not to play with us anymore after winning state. I don't know what to believe, but either one of those rumors could be true, knowing the way those people at the game were acting.

It scares me to think what could happen to me, even if I don't talk or act like Peter. Before I shut him out, Eddie told me that from the time he was a little kid, his daddy always told him to know who the bad men are and to stay away from them. Said he had friends who didn't say a thing to a white man and still got lynched.

I rub my throat and wonder. Then I think about all those white folks I've been trying to get jobs from. Maybe I'd have better luck with a colored business.

The first place I try is Pappy's Sweet Shoppe and Laundromat, a favorite hangout spot for the kids at school. When I get there, I see the small glass case filled with all kinds of penny candy—red-hot dollars, jawbreakers, and Bazookas. Moon Pies, Zero bars, and Bit 'o Honey.

With all that candy around, I might not stay skinny, and I need to be small to play my position. In the back of the store is where Pappy keeps the washers and dryers. I recall the time Eddie brought me here so he could fish nickels and dimes out of them for lunch money. That was back before I learned I was colored, and things went south for Eddie and me.

"Come on," said Eddie, directing me to the dryers. "I have to get enough money to eat lunch tomorrow." He pulled opened each dryer door and leaned in so all you could see was the back of his trousers. I just stood by and watched him squirm around in the oversized cylinders searching for lost change.

"Aren't you going to help?" He asked, looking at me sideways. "I got to clean every one of these before supper time..."

The memory makes me smile, but Eddie and me haven't said a word to each other since the awards ceremony. How do you make up with someone you practically threw out of your house? And who'd want to make up with somebody who treated them that way? I shut him out that first night I found out I was colored, and it feels like every time I've tried to open back up, I've just made things worse. If it turns out he's right about Peter, he'll probably never forgive me for doubting him. It'll be a long time before Eddie and I can be friends again, if ever.

"Anything I can help you with?" says a tall, light-skinned man with kinky red hair and broad shoulders. I don't answer, staring at his freckles. I'd never seen a colored kid with freckles until I got to Douglass, but seeing them on a man throws me even more.

"Are you Pappy?" I manage to ask, embarrassed. I know he caught me staring.

"Who wants to know?"

"Well, I—I was wondering if...if you needed any help around here."

He frowns. "I'm Pappy. What kind of help can a scrawny kid like you offer?"

I clear my throat and walk a little closer. "Well, sir, I could keep your candy shelves neat—"

"Yeah, and eat up all my profits. What else?" His frown turns into a smile, like we're playing a game.

"I could clean up the floors around the Laundromat, and—"

"And steal all the change out of the machines while you're at it." He leans against the glass case. "I already got a kid who comes 'round to do that, so if it's work you're looking for, I'm afraid you got the wrong man. Try up the street a ways, at Rogers' Sandwich Shoppe. He might need some help."

With that, Pappy shows me to the door. I stand outside for a minute to think. Why would a colored business give me a job when they can give one to a colored kid? A kid who looks colored, I mean.

That gives me an idea.

As soon as I make it to Rogers' Sandwich Shoppe, I go right in and tell the man behind the counter the truth.

"Excuse me, sir, I may not look it, but I'm colored, and I—"

The small lunch spot bursts into laughter.

"You? Colored?" one man says.

"What you tryin' to pull, little man?" says a woman holding a baby.

I look around the place. It's a small building, sort of like he converted a house. It has a counter with some stools. Card tables line the wall with fold-up chairs. A few people are sitting and eating, while about six or seven are in line to get their order. All of them are smiling, snickering, or talking loud about me, as if I'm not here.

Then a man comes from the kitchen area, wiping his hands on a towel.

"What's going on out here?"

"This white boy says he's colored," says the man I thought was Mr. Rogers.

The others nod, and some laugh.

"I'm Rogers. What you want in here, son?"

At first I don't understand the question until I look around. I'm the only person in here who looks white, and even though I'm not, they don't know that.

"I *am* colored, Mr. Rogers. I'm just real, real light, that's all, and I need an after-school job, or else me and my mama's gonna starve."

"Ha," says a man behind me. "You got the nerve to come in here amongst all of us and start yammering about not having nothing to eat? Excuse me, Mr. White Boy, but I believe we got the market cornered on that one—"

"Tell him about it," says the man next to him. He looks mean in his black knit cap and green Army jacket. He has a scar across his face from nose to jaw.

"And if you know what's good for you, boy, you'll get outta here while the gettin' is good," says another. He's holding a fried bologna sandwich, and it sure smells good. The menu says it's Rogers' specialty. The smell of the crisp, warm meat with mayonnaise slathered on top makes my mouth water.

By now, everyone is fussing and complaining about white people this and white people that. I don't know what to do, so I leave as fast as I can, their voices bouncing off my back.

"Hey there," someone calls from behind me. I'm afraid to turn around, so I walk faster. The voice calls again.

"Young fella, wait a minute."

This time the voice sounds friendly, so I turn back to find Mr. Rogers walking towards me. When he reaches me, he's huffing and puffing, his belly pushing against his long T-shirt and full-length apron.

"Why you lookin' for a job 'round here, son?"

I search his eyes for something decent before I give him my answer. They look beat down, like they're ready to close up and quit.

"Well, yes, sir. Some of the kids over at my school, Douglass, say you might be looking for some after-school help, and, well, I was trying to get a job, if I could."

Mr. Rogers rubs his forehead with the lower edge of his apron.

"I hate to disappoint you, son, but the truth is, I may not be able to keep the shop open much longer. City's trying to buy up this land for the college there yonder, and that means we goin' to have to get out. With integration coming fast and furious, folks in power figure there ain't no need for small colored businesses no more."

"Why?"

"The city calls it progress. Folks get to thinking, 'Why do you need two hot dog stands when we can all go to the good one?' Next thing you know, white businesses got your customers and your customers' money. Before you know it, you can't keep your doors open. I can see it coming. When colored shoppers get inside a white business, they'll think it's better just because they never got in before. And that'll be the end of that."

After listening to Mr. Rogers tell his story, I feel bad that I asked for a job when he's about to lose his business. I remember Eddie saying that colored folks don't want integration; they want equality. Now I'm finally starting to realize what he meant.

"It's OK," I tell him. "I hope they don't close your business."

"Look, you wait right here for a minute. Now don't go away."

It's the breezy part of the day in Montgomery, and the magnolia trees are in bloom. Their perfume reminds me of the ones we had in our yard on Boultier. The house I'll never go back to. I keep my hands in my pockets as I catch sight of Mr. Rogers coming back down the street. He has a white paper bag in his hand.

"Take this home for you and your mama," he says. "And may the Lord bless you and me."

I smile and thank him. After he gets a good distance away, I look inside the bag, and it hits me: the charred, sweet smell of bologna and mayonnaise. I can't wait to dig in, so I grab half the sandwich and eat it as I walk.

I take my time going home, thinking about what Mr. Rogers said about losing his business. Maybe it's the juicy sandwich affecting my judgment, but it would be a shame to lose a place like his because of integration. What's going to come along and take its place?

Something has to be done. I finish off the last corner of my sandwich and lick my fingers. *I just don't know what.*

All the rallies and protests seem to focus on letting colored folks into white stores. There's nothing focused on the black businesses.

That's when it hits me. Maybe I can protest the closing of these stores the same as they're doing to get into white ones? I decide that when I make up with Eddie, that's the first thing we're gonna do. In fact, why wait? I'm gonna head over to Eddie's right now and get my friend back.

I speed up my pace a yard or two, then the spring in my step fades away. Who am I fooling? As long as people hate, things will never be equal and sure not fair.

10

———————

When I get home, the rail that connects to the steps on the side of our building is bent all the way to the ground, barely hanging onto its hinges. That's just the way I feel too. Beat down. Knocked out of kilter. Mama and I are still struggling. Something inside tells me to give up. Forget trying to find a job. Mama and I will be on welfare forever. As long as I'm a colored boy, my white skin will never make a bit of difference.

I know that for sure now.

I get to the door of our apartment. The TV's on inside. Mama rarely watches TV except Sunday nights when I turn on *Ed Sullivan*. I open the door, and sitting square in front of me at our kitchen table is a woman. A colored woman. I recognize her as one of the maids that used to come by. My eyes dart around.

"Where's my Mama?"

The woman stands but doesn't come near. Her face full of worry.

"Your mama's in the hospital."

"What hospital? What happened?"

"She had a bad attack while we was sitting here talking, so I called emergency."

I head for the door. She takes hold of my shoulders and turns me around.

"Mark, she left me here to tell you not to come."

"Why?"

"They's keeping her overnight is all. I fixed you some supper over there on the stove. She says to tell you not to worry. To eat and do your homework."

I don't know what to say except, "Yes, ma'am."

She grabs her purse off the table and holds it with both hands. "I have to go see about my own youngins. You gon be all right, son?"

I nod.

She walks to the door. "She gonna have someone call you."

I nod again, and she leaves, closing the door behind her.

I sit at the kitchen table and let out a long sigh. I hate that I can't do anything to help. If I'd been here instead of out looking for a job, I could've gone with her. She wouldn't be alone right now. Worse, she's gonna be mighty upset when them medical bills come. We can hardly pay for living from day to day, let alone a visit to the hospital.

I slam my fist on the table. It's not fair. None of it is.

When the phone rings I run to it, thinking it must be the hospital. I snatch the receiver off the cradle and respond. It's Billy.

What in the heck does he want?

"Hey Lawson, how's tricks?"

"Look, Billy, I'm expecting an important phone call so I need to clear the line—"

"Ah, Lawson, who'd want to be calling you except me?" Billy chuckles.

"I'm serious—"

"OK, OK. Don't get sore. I was just wanting to know if you and I could, you know, bury the hatchet."

Am I hearing him right?

"You know, let bygones be bygones and all of that nonsense. Whaddya say?"

I shake my head listening to him try to sound like his big brother Matt.

"Are ya there, Lawson?"

Now I'm pacing the floor.

Why does he want to be my pal all of a sudden? What's in it for him? There's gotta be a catch.

"I'm here, Billy, but I don't understand—"

"What's there to understand?" He bellows, "I'm trying to give you a break. Don't you get it? A break Mark—"

A break. I sure could use one. No. A job. That's what I really need.

"I'm offering you a chance to get back in my good graces, Lawson. If you know what I mean—"

I'm sweating now. I run my hand through my hair and pace again, pulling the phone cord all over the room.

I can't do this. I can't get buddy-buddy with Billy. It's the last thing I need to do.

He hates colored people. HATES them.

"Look, Billy, I-I—"

"Listen to me, Lawson, you need a job, right? My family's got jobs. Those poor-ass niggers can't get you a job, and I know you've tried. The word's on the street—"

Why is he doing this to me? If Mama wasn't so sick and we weren't so poor...

"Look, Lawson, why don't you come hang out with Hank and me tonight? There's a big college game over at State—"

I can't do this. I can't.

Billy is like a snake that coils itself around you when you're least able to defend yourself, and then he squeezes the life out of you. But something inside me wants to say yes. Something bigger than my pride. Something that keeps nagging at me to do wrong even if I don't want to.

"Let me be straight with you, Mark. I—I kinda need a good friend right now. I mean, I got Hank, but you know... Ray is gone, and...and Matt—"

I admit I do feel sorry for him—losing Ray and Matt going to Vietnam.

"Come on, whaddya say?"

"Uh...OK."

"Great. I'll pick you up in the Corvette at eight."

Click.

I hold the phone away from my ear and stare at it. The curled-up cord leading to the wall looks just like a serpent.

I can't believe what just happened. I must be out of my mind; otherwise, I would have hung right up on him. I can't explain why I agreed to spend time with a viper.

Then again, maybe he's changing. And maybe, if I can show Billy this race thing is all wrong, maybe I'll still have a chance to give Mama all the things I want to give her. I've been striking out on jobs lately, and, well, I guess I half-believe it's still possible. That maybe soon my race won't matter. That maybe soon I can just be Mark Lawson instead of somebody who needs a description after his name. Maybe he'll even give back my Mantle.

Billy said on the phone that he and Hank want me to go with them to a State game. I've never been to a college game, and I'm getting excited. I'm desperate to feel good for once. I'm tired of standing on the fringes of my own life looking in like an outsider. Just this once I'm gonna allow myself to own what's still in my heart: the belief that we can all get along. I have to. Besides, Billy may be my last chance.

———

A few hours later, the hospital calls and says Mama's doing better, and she'll be released tomorrow. They'll arrange for someone to bring her home.

When Billy finally comes to pick me up, he's driving a brand new Corvette convertible. It's sweet and white with gleaming rims. It's the hottest car I've ever seen, all shined up in Turtle Wax. Mama's convertible pops into my head. If I had had that job a long time ago, she'd a never lost it, and I'd be riding in style just like this. That thought makes my decision to hang with Billy even clearer. It's my time to shine.

"Yours, Billy? Sweet."

"Ah, it's just a car. Now you see here, Lawson, the minute we get to that game, you just follow my lead, you hear? Everything's gonna be just fine."

Right away Billy revs the engine and peels out of the parking lot. We pick up Hank and speed across town. It's a gas feeling the wind all around me and the town flying by in flashes. My head's spinning like a hippie high. 'Course, I'd never try drugs, but I can imagine floating on some crazy carefree cloud. That's how I feel tonight—reckless.

Billy turns down Carter Hill Road. But there's no college field down this way except our ball field at Huntingdon, and they don't have a game tonight. We get closer to my neck of the woods, and that sick feeling I had when I was on the phone with Billy comes back full force. I should've trusted my gut. I know Billy's history, which makes it easy to just about map out the rest of the evening.

We pull into the back lot of Alabama State College. Billy parks in a dark spot behind the garbage bins. He gets out. I hesitate. He knows why.

"So Lawson, are you in, or not?"

"What's the point?" I ask. "Why you gotta do this? I just don't get it. Is this what fun is to you? Beating up coloreds? Why can't you get past this race thing? Why you gotta be prejudiced?"

I stare at Billy, but I see only emptiness in his eyes.

Hank starts for me, but Billy's arm keeps him away. Instead, he takes Hank's place, stepping so close to me I can feel his breath traveling up my nose.

"Either you stick with us out here tonight, or you don't stick with us at all. You get me, Lawson?" Then he reels me in. "Or don't you want to work for my daddy?"

I know Coach Justice is the richest man in town and has powerful friends. All he has to do is say the word, and I can finally take care of Mama the way she deserves. Coach Justice even said I had a good raisin'. I know it's a long shot, but maybe if I give Billy this one night, things will finally start to turn around for me.

I swallow hard, forcing my better judgment down deep.

"What do you want me to do?"

We walk the campus for ten or fifteen minutes looking for someone out alone. Someone they can jump. The sky is black as coal, and the night air is hot and sticky. I'm nervous as a possum crossing the highway.

A young man is coming toward us. He's carrying some books. He looks like an easy target.

"Just keep cool and follow my lead," Billy whispers.

As soon as we get up close to the guy, lights flash on us. I throw my hands in front of my eyes. I can't see anything but a form.

"What's the meaning of this?" says a man who must be a night watchman, his flashlight still shining on us.

He's dark and tall and burly. He steps right up to Billy, making him look like a shrimp.

"We—we're not do-ing nothing," Billy says with a trembling voice, and I squint to make sure that's Billy Justice talking, the big bad bully who hates coloreds. In front of this big man, he's nothing but a wuss. In the meantime, Hank is keeping his mouth shut. At least he's got that much sense.

"I suggest you get your pale asses off this property before I have to do something I'll regret."

Billy backs away from the man, bumping into Hank and me. The man stands firm. His muscular arms crossed.

Billy turns and jumps into the car. I barely get in before he takes off.

Riding through town, nobody says a word. Then Billy starts up again.

"I got an idea. Let's go shoot out some streetlights." He reaches into the glove compartment and pulls out what I hope is a BB gun. He holds it high. "You got yours, Hank?"

"You betcha."

They don't bother asking me.

We keep riding. This trip doesn't feel so good. No excitement over the wind or the clouds or any of that. I just close my eyes and imagine the tongue-lashing I'll get when Mama finds out what I did tonight.

Billy's convertible shoots down Perry Avenue. And once we get to the VA Hospital, my insides ache. This is Eddie's spot. The place he comes to pick pecans. Every couple of weeks his mother brings him here, and the two of them fill brown paper bags to the brim and then sell them to the pecan man, so-called. I close my eyes and wish I could go back to those few weeks after Eddie got chosen for pitcher, before I discovered the truth about my daddy. Things were easier then.

"Come on," Billy yells, running toward the building that seems monstrous in the moonlight. It's clear he has his sights on the spotlights dotted all around the grounds.

PING

PING

PING

One light out. Then two. Then three.

"Billy, we're gonna get in trouble," I tell him, but he just keeps shooting.

Hank runs to the back of the building to do his dirty work. The property is so spread out there's no way I can keep up with both of them.

I hide underneath one of the towering pecan trees and wait for them to finish. It's a good idea at first. Then comes a low sound like a tornado warning. It grows louder and louder, making my heart beat faster and faster. Someone set off the alarm.

I jump to my feet, but I don't know which way to run. My legs, my eyes, and my will to survive search like crazy for Billy and Hank. But nobody's around. Nobody but me.

I panic and run. Then I see the two of them heading to the car, just as the police sirens wail closer and closer.

"Hey, wait for me," I yell as they speed off into the darkness.

Two police cars rush the sidewalk, bright lights shining. I freeze.

"Put your hands on your head, son," the officer says, holding his pistol at his side.

One of them pulls me over to the car and cuffs me. He has a big build that reminds me of Matt Dillon on *Gunsmoke*. Has a face like him too, only his never smiles. At least Sheriff Dillon smiles sometimes.

"What's your name?"

"Mark Lawson."

"Where do you live?"

"7802 Eastman Road."

The officers look at each other.

"You better tell us the truth, boy; you don't live on Eastman, and you know it."

Sweat is pouring over me like a morning rain. At that point it's a crapshoot as to whether I'll be dead or alive tomorrow. If I tell them I'm colored, who knows what they might do, especially if Eddie was right about what happened to Peter.

"1628 Boultier Drive," I lie, but to him, only coloreds live on Eastman.

"Who's your daddy?"

"He's dead."

"And your mother?"

"Sarah Lawson."

"Ya oughta know better being on this side of town boy."

"What are you gonna do with me?"

My heart is racing, and my palms sweat.

"What do you think we oughta do? You out here breaking the law and all?"

"It—it wasn't me, sir."

"Well, can't say I see nobody else out here."

"But the convertible. Didn't you see it?"

"Nope, can't say I did. You better come with us."

"But it was right there as you were pulling up. I can't believe you didn't see it."

"The less you flap your lips, there sonny, the longer you'll have 'em. Now git in the car."

The officer swings open the patrol car door and orders me to sit—his palm pushes down on my head.

The first time I've ever been in a police car, and right at that moment I swear I'll be a green-eyed gopher before it ever happens again. The ride ties my nerves up in knots. Mama's never gonna forgive me for this, and Coach Collier might just kick me off the team.

The cuffs rub against my wrists, making them sweat and itch. My arms go stiff from having them forced behind my back. My forehead hits the seat in front of me every time we hit a bump, and my back bangs against the cuffs at sudden stops.

Neither one of the officers ever asks me how I'm doing. Guess neither one of them cares. It crosses my mind that maybe they know I'm colored, which is why they let the others go.

Coloreds and cops aren't very happy with each other these days on account of integration. And although I was young, I remember how bad it used to be. Just a few years ago they'd beat a colored sure as looking at 'em—a lot of times for no reason. Like that march last year in Selma. They did it just because. Thinking of it now, I can feel a heat rise in me. I'm angry at myself. Mad at my race: the white half of it.

"OK, son, this is your new home 'til somebody comes and gets you." They pull me out of the car and take me into the station.

"Got a live one, have you?" says the man behind the glass window.

"Shootin' out streetlights down the VA," the officer tells him.

"Got the gun?" asks the man.

"Naw, but that's what he was doin'."

"I-I don't even own a BB gun."

"Look, son, we knows how you kids are. You see us coming, and you throw the darn things in the bushes. We'll find it tomorrow."

"But I'm telling the truth—"

"Just calm down boy 'fore I get angry and have to do something I'll regret."

My instincts tell my mouth to keep quiet. Eddie once said that the police always treat coloreds like they're guilty until proven innocent. Seems he's been right about everything.

I sit there for what seems like hours, but no one shows up, probably because no one can. Not Mama and not Coach Collier. That's when I overhear the man behind the glass talking to his partner. They look over at me as if seeing me in a whole new light. They know. No mistaking it now. They know.

The man behind the glass comes out and toward me. His face grows pasty.

"I'll be damned." He turns to the officer who brought me in. He's standing in front of me, too.

"He's a niggra," the first man says, like he's trying to convince himself. "Says so right here on this report."

The officer looks pitiful, the way folks do when they got to put a dog down but their conscience bothers them.

"Think we oughta call that Big Brother-colored guy to come get him?"

"Goshay? Sure, why not? He's always trying to help these delinquents. What's his mother say?"

"Sh' ain't home. No answer."

"I told you she was in the hospital," I say.

"Guess you better call 'im then. Oh, and put on another pot, will ya? Gonna be a long night."

I wiggle my finger in my ear searching for wax, both of them in fact, 'cause I must've heard him wrong. Goshay? Does he mean another Goshay? Coming to get me? Has to be a mistake. But when a big dark man walks in wearing a Civil War cap, I darn near wet myself.

I slam my lids shut and squeeze real tight, knowing that when I open them someone else'll be standing there. Nope. It's Mr. Goshay, Eddie's dad.

"Good ol' Goshay, thanks for coming out," the man behind the glass says.

"Where is he?" says Eddie's father, peeping around one corner and then the next.

"We got 'em in the office over there, see?" The other man points me out. "He's been waiting quite a while."

Our eyes meet, and recognition dawns on his face.

"That's why we called you," says the officer. "We can't reach his mama, and the boy ain't got no record, so we figured you could talk some sense into him like you do all those other wayward niggras that end up in here."

The officer smiles as he digs through a wrinkled bag and pulls out a wad of snuff. I see Mr. Goshay's jaw tighten.

"So you ain't keepin' him here, like the others?"

"Now, how you 'spect it's gonna look if somebody was to see we got a boy as white as him in jail?" the officer says through a cheek full of tobacco. "You just take the little niggra home and mind your business like a good boy."

He chews and stares hard at Eddie's father. Mr. Goshay goes to the man behind the glass, signs something, and then walks over to me.

"Come on, son."

We ride back in the Delta 88 he and Eddie drove to the state championship. I'd read about the car and knew it could go way faster than the creep-along speed it's doing. It feels strange sitting next to Mr. Goshay when I can't seem to get half as close to his son.

He's silent, and so am I. As we head back, I can't help but steal a glance at him every now and then, trying to figure it out. How can he take out the time to help me when Eddie and I don't even speak? I want to thank him, but I can't find the words. He looks over at me once or twice, too. Catches me rubbing my hands together, nervous.

He stops in front of my building and doesn't say anything about where I live. I hurry out.

"Listen here, they said your mama's in the hospital. You got a key?"

"Yes, sir."

He sits in the car with the window rolled down and just looks at me for a minute. "Come here, son."

I step closer and lean in.

"You know what just happened back there, don't you?'

"Not really, sir."

"They know you ain't white, same as I do, but 'cause you look white, they didn't keep you. You understand?"

"I can't say that I do."

Mr. Goshay looks away and takes a deep breath. "You got two choices, son. You can either live life the way you look or live it the way you are. It's up to you. But one thing's for sure, you gotta decide which it's gonna be 'cause you can't be both. Not in this town. Not in this world, even."

I lower my head because I don't know how to respond to him. I don't see myself as both or either. On the one hand, I don't understand why I have to choose, but on the other hand, I know *exactly* why, and neither allows me to make the best choice for *me*. It's all for somebody else's benefit. I push up from the door.

"You sure you gon be all right by yourself?"

"Yes, sir. Thank you for bringing me home."

"You stay away from them police, ya hear?"

"Yes, sir."

He waves and drives off. I stay outside for a minute or two thinking about this night and how stupid I've been. Mama would be real upset if she ever found out what happened. As I walk toward the apartment building, I look up at the dark sky and the bright yellow moon.

Is there really someone up there listening?

I watch, and I whisper, "If you can hear me, please bring my Mama home tomorrow. If you do, I promise I won't ever act like I don't appreciate the boy you made me. Mama says you don't make mistakes, so could you teach me not to make 'em too? If you're listening, I mean."

I gaze up there so long my neck hurts, so I rub it and climb the stairs, knowing that either I'm gonna be happy when I wake up the next morning, or I'll be sad. I just hope I wasn't talking to the wrong father.

11

$\mathcal{M}$ama comes home early in the morning, and I don't know it until she wakes me with a shake of my arm. Says the doctors called in a prescription for her, and she needs me to go down to Miller's Grocery to pick it up.

It's Saturday, and I really don't want to go downtown, especially since I heard there's supposed to be a march down there today. I wish Mama could find a drugstore closer to home, but she says Miller's is the cheapest, and the new Medicaid she's on only allows her to get it at approved locations. That's what I hate about this assistance we're getting. They make stuff hard that should be easy.

I bet Eddie'll be at this march. Even if he keeps his mouth shut, it'd be just my luck to get recognized by some *other* kid from my school who could *also* be marching. I don't think Mr. Miller knows I'm colored, and I don't want him to refuse Mama's medicine.

Ever since the day I stole that apple, I've tried to avoid seeing Mr. Miller at the store. Maybe I'm just being stupid. After all, it's been six months since I was expelled, and it's not like the whole town knew about it. Most of the people on the Southside don't even come down here to these businesses, especially since they have a drugstore that's closer. I'll just do what I usually do: get Mama's prescriptions and get out as soon as I can.

After I get off the bus, I walk in slow and quiet, like I usually do, and I keep my eye out for signs of marchers outside the store.

"Well, hey there, young fella," says Mr. Miller. He flashes me a wide smile. "How's it going?"

"Just fine, sir," I say.

He sees the prescription in my hand. I usually give it to the druggist. I hand it over, and he takes it to the back. He returns in a few minutes.

"Andy'll get this filled right away."

Mr. Miller puts his arm around my shoulder, and we walk to the counter where he keeps a big jar of dill pickles, beef jerky, and other stuff he can sell to people when they check out. There's donuts, ladyfingers, and elephant ears in the glass case, and some empty barrels turned upside down to use as display places. Most of his sale items show up there. In the back is where the pharmacist mixes up the compounds and things for all the patients.

"Your mother's not doing so well, eh?" says Mr. Miller, with a concerned face.

"No, sir," I admit.

Mama's been taking these pills for a while, but to me, they don't seem to be working. Her diet's improving, thanks to the help from our neighbors, but she's not better.

"Well, the doctors know best," he says. "The only thing you can do is to be there when she needs you. That'll give her comfort."

"Yes, sir."

"Did you ever find a job? I know you were looking."

"No, sir," I say, lowering my head. I forgot I told him about that the day I stole the apple. "Nobody's hiring, I guess. Well, nobody my age anyway."

I keep my eye on the storefront window. If those marchers show up, I plan to get lost.

"You expecting somebody, son?"

I immediately look at him. "Oh, no. No, I was just looking to see if it's raining. I heard it was gonna rain." The longer I talk to Mr. Miller, the less comfortable I get. "You think that prescription's ready yet?" I ask, staring toward the back of the store.

"Let me check."

While he's gone, I look outside again. I don't see anyone, and that's a relief. Maybe the marchers heard it was going to rain, too.

"Here you go, son. And tell your Ma to take just one pill a day; that way she won't run out so quickly."

"I'll tell her." I take the white paper bag and head for the door.

"Mark, wait a second." Mr. Miller joins me at the store entrance. "How would you like to come *here* and work?"

My heart starts thumping. "Really? Gee, I sure would, Mr. Miller, but I—"

Right away I feel unsure about my answer.

Do I really want to work here, without him knowing I'm colored?

My brain is banging inside my head.

I need a job, and he is offering.

"Good. I could use someone to help me around here, to set up displays and keep track of the inventory." He leans close to me, "just in case some kid comes along trying to steal my apples."

He smiles and rustles my hair. My smile's not so wide. I push my hair back in place.

"Sorry, I forget you older kids don't like your hair mussed up."

"Yes, sir. Uh, when did you need me to start?"

"Well, with schools about to open, I don't want to horn in on your homework time—"

"Oh, well, I could come on the weekends?" I offer.

"That sounds fine. How about every Saturday, from nine to five? Does that work?"

"It sure does. Thanks, Mr. Miller." I grab the door handle.

"Mark?"

"Sir?"

"Don't you want to know the pay?"

"Oh, uh, sure."

"Does a dollar an hour sound good to you?"

I'm so full of air I cough. He pats my back. "Yes, sir."

In my head I calculate it. I'd be making eight dollars a day, thirty-two dollars a month. Maybe forty, in long months. Mama could do a lot with forty dollars. I grab Mr. Miller's hand and shake it as firm as I can, like a man.

He smiles. "I'm sure you'll earn every penny."

"Thanks again," I say, and push through the door.

Out on the sidewalk, I want to let out a great big yell. I'm still not sure this was the right thing for me to do, not telling him my color. But I can't worry about what hasn't happened. Pa always said, "Leave tomorrow's worries for tomorrow." That's what I aim to do.

While I'm waiting to catch the bus across town, I see Eddie on the opposite side of the street. He's with those marchers again, handing out signs. A TV camera is there, too. Right now there's nothing he or anyone else could do to ruin my good news, but I'm still concerned. I don't want them protesting in front of my new job, even if they feel they got a right to. I can't help but wonder when these marches are going to stop. The way Peter talks, they aren't doing a lot of good anyway. It's like Mr. Rogers said, they just want to get into to the "good" store.

I decide to get away from here before Eddie sees me. Besides, Mama needs her medicine, and I want to give her the good news.

———

It's my first day as a stock boy at Miller's Grocery. I can hardly believe it. I got a real job. Who knows where this could lead? Today I'm a stock boy, but next year I could be a sales clerk. Yep, I'm feeling on top of the world, and I owe it all to Mama. If it wasn't for her choosing to send her prescriptions to Mr. Miller, I'd never even know about the job. Though I hate that she has to take those pills, at least they make her feel better until a cure comes along.

I wear a white apron, just like Mr. Miller, and I keep a pencil behind my ear, too. After a few Saturdays are under my belt, the work comes easy to me. I sweep the back room and keep track of what sells from the carts outside. When there's a sale, I set up displays on top of the old barrels. I haven't taken inventory yet, but I figure he's going to let me do that soon, since he says I have a good head for numbers.

Besides hiring me, Mr. Miller also has a new assistant. His name is Will. Didn't catch his last name. He's younger than Mr. Miller, about Melissa's age. Tall and willowy, like a sudden wind would blow him clean away. He runs the place whenever Mr. Miller can't make it. He takes advantage of that, too: a few times I caught him reading girlie magazines when he was supposed to be working.

While taking the trash out back, I see a nice red sports car in the parking lot. It must be Will's. It's a '65 Mustang with thick white racing stripes. Mr. Miller must be paying Will a sweet salary. I put down the trash bags and check it out. I lean close to the window on the driver's side. It's packed with options: an AM/FM radio, an ashtray, and a lighter. It even has red bucket seats. I walk around to check out the wheels.

"Man, I haven't seen a car like this since Becky Gilmore's brother brought her to school in—"

I back away from the car and take a quick look around.

No, it can't be.

I get back inside and try to act normal around Will.

"I was about to send out the National Guard after you, kid," says Will, ringing up a sale. The customer smiles at me then tips his hat at Will.

"Thanks for coming in," Will says to the man. A white man.

That's when I start to think: up until now, I never really noticed that only white people come in the store. Not one colored person. I want to believe it's just a coincidence, but if it's on purpose, I'm dead meat, especially if Will turns out to be Becky's big brother.

I move over to the shelf of canned goods and pretend to arrange them better.

"So how you liking it here so far?" Will asks me.

"Fine," I say, keeping my back to him. The day Becky's brother dropped her off, I know he saw me and Bosley standing on the sidewalk admiring the car. I didn't see his face. I hope he doesn't remember mine.

"What school do you go to?" he asks, still behind the counter. But before I have a chance to answer, the chime of the door sends him off to wait on another customer.

I go back to the office to see if Mr. Miller has anything for me to do. I aim to stay clear of Will. If he finds out that Becky knows me, my job is out the window.

———

I'm getting nervous about all this and eager to talk things out with somebody, so I try mending fences with Eddie again. I've learned a lot about myself since that Board of Education letter arrived, and I just want things to get back to normal between us. It's been too long.

In the hall. At lunch. No time seems to be a good one for us to talk things out. I want him to know where I stand as far as my feelings about being colored, and I'll have to say it's taking some time for me to come to terms with it. Truly come to terms. It's my honest answer. He knows me too well for me to give him the jive talk.

No sooner do I go over what I want to say to him, there he is, standing by his locker.

"Hey Eddie," I say.

I rush over, but I'm careful not to crowd him. At first he doesn't look up. Just keeps fiddling with the lock combination.

"Those things are kind of tricky sometimes," I say. "I have to jiggle mine."

"Why'd you go hanging out with Billy?" he asks me, still concentrating on the lock. He throws me off guard. I remain silent. "What? You didn't think my dad would tell me?" he asks with a smirk on his face. "We talk about everything."

He looks hard at me.

"I made a mistake, OK?"

"You sure did, and to think my dad had to bail you out of jail is pretty sad. A colored boy who thinks he's white getting help from a colored man who *knows* who he is."

"You're wrong, Eddie. I didn't ask for your dad's help, though I'm grateful. I learned my own lesson that night, and I don't need you to rub it in."

How did this conversation end up about Billy instead of us?

"Eddie, I came over here to ask you to be my friend again. I didn't mean to push you away and—"

"Forget it, Mark," he says, finally getting the lock to open. "I'm not interested in being friends with somebody who doesn't even know who he is. No, let me take that back. Somebody who doesn't want to *be* who he is." He slams the locker door and walks away.

The last thing I wanted to do was have an argument. Heck, it all happened so fast I hardly understood what kind of argument we actually had. He could have at least heard me out. Now I feel like I'm even further away from making up with Eddie than I was before. Trouble is, he still thinks I'm trying to be different. On that score he's dead wrong.

12

———————

elissa's home again. This time she drove a car. Says it belongs to a friend at school whose father owns a used car lot. All she has to do is keep it gassed up. She's working at night and on the weekends to help ease the burden on Mama and me. At least she's not calling me every week asking for pocket change. I plan to save for a new mitt and maybe even a bat. But for now I'm doing my best to make sure the cupboards aren't bare.

We still haven't settled our differences. When it comes to making up with girls, I never know the right things to say. When Mama tells Melissa and me to wash the Sunday dishes because she needs to lie down, I hope nothing ignorant comes up and spills out of my mouth.

I'm watching my sister work, as if for the first time. She's all grown up. Today she looks a lot like Mama. Her blonde hair curls at the ends. It looks neater than it did the last time I saw her; it kind of bounces whenever she flips it out of her way. Her pale skin glows as smooth as butter and turns pinkish orange at her cheeks.

"What is it?" she says, with the same tone Mama uses to scold me. She's staring before I notice I've been caught in a daze.

"Huh?" I say, like I don't know what she means.

Melissa sighs and returns to washing dishes. I keep drying, trying to figure out what to say, still not really sure if I should say anything at all. I've never apologized to her before, and I don't know how to start.

"Kids," Mama calls from the back room. "You finished yet? I'm gonna try to get to the church social before too long."

"Almost, Mama," Melissa says. "If Mark would stop daydreaming and dry." She gives me two eyes full of "so there" and turns up her nose.

Same old Melissa.

"I *am* drying," I say loud enough for Mama to hear.

Melissa puts the last dish on my side of the sink, rinses her hands, and turns to leave. I grab her arm before she can walk away.

"What's wrong with you?" she asks.

"I want to talk," I say, surprised I mustered up that much. "Please?"

"What about? I promised Mama I'd go to the social with her, and I've got to get ready."

"You can go over later. I'll go with you—"

"You? At a church social?" she laughs.

"I really need to talk to you."

Melissa takes one step back and eyes me from head to toe. If she thinks I'm kidding around, she doesn't say so. "OK, but make it quick."

I nod and head outside. When she comes out, we sit on the cramped fire escape. Melissa leans back and supports herself with the palms of her hands. I stare straight ahead.

"Well?" she asks.

"How did it feel?" I turn my head slightly toward her and let out a long sigh. "How did you really feel about it...when you first heard? This life of ours, I mean. And I'm not talking about hanging out with coloreds and whites or nothing like that. I want to know how you did it... inside."

She sits up and dusts off her hands. "Seriously? You sure you're ready to learn what you think you already know?"

"I guess so."

She stares straight ahead this time, as if trying to figure out how to tell me something too painful to say.

"Well, if you're not fooling and really want to know, it was just as hard for me to learn about it as it was for you, except I heard it from Daddy.

We were in the General Store in Melrose, Louisiana. It was a little while after you were born, before we came to Alabama. I was about seven, I think, and this man had been staring at me from behind the flour sacks. He seemed like he tried not to stare, but each time my eyes ventured over in that direction, there he was, gawking at me like he couldn't stop himself. Finally, he came right up to Daddy and asked him.

He said, "Strange how your girl can stand the sun. Why, as soon as my two get a little light on them, their skin turns beet red."

Daddy wasn't too happy with the remark, and I guess that made the man curious.

"You sure she yorn?" he asked.

That's when other folks stopped buying and shopping and stared. You should have seen Daddy's face. I swear it also turned beet red. I could even feel anger in his hand 'cause I was holding it, and the heat went all through me. On the way home, he said it was time he explained some things.

"That's when he told me," Melissa says. "Of course, I didn't understand, but afterward I paid more attention to folks when they looked at me. Guess that man spread the word, and you know how small Melrose is. Some were so busy staring they'd bump into things, trying to decide what I was. Some just shunned me so whatever I had wouldn't rub off on them, I guess." Melissa sighs long and hard. "I tried to ignore it, but I knew being mulatto made me different, even from kids who looked like me. I cried when the white kids didn't want to play with me. So I spent most of my time with the coloreds. But even some of them didn't want me around."

Melissa turns to me. Her eyes filled with sadness, like she's seven all over again.

"I sure know that feeling," I say. "Before I got my job, I hung out with a racist kid one night and got arrested—"

"Arrested? For what?"

"Something they did, but one of my teammates' dads got me out and brought me home. I felt real bad."

"Does Mama know?"

"No. And I ain't telling her either."

"What were you doing with that boy anyway?"

"Guess I wanted to be accepted, like you. I also wanted his help getting a job, but I went about it the wrong way and with the wrong person."

"Well, I'll be out of school soon, and I can send some more money. If you can hang on to that job a bit longer, that would be good."

I lower my eyes. "There's just one thing."

"What's that?"

"He doesn't know."

"Who doesn't know what?"

"My boss."

I look up, and I'm not surprised to see her reaction. Like I'm a sellout.

"Mark, why didn't you tell him? My God! And in Montgomery too!"

"Thanks for being supportive."

"I'm sorry, but you know what I mean. You could get hurt if he finds out the truth."

"You think I haven't thought about that? And what's worse is the assistant manager is the brother of a girl I knew at my old school."

"What?"

"He doesn't seem to remember seeing me; I'm counting on that."

"Mark, you be careful, you hear me? You could jeopardize everything. Think of Mama."

I wrap my fingers around a railing. Melissa puts her hand on my back.

"Just pray about it."

I look up at Melissa 'cause she sounds just like Mama saying that. I change the subject before I get teary-eyed.

"This whole thing has been so hard." I shake my head over and over.

"Oh, Mark, I'm sorry this has been so rough on you, but you can't let others decide who you are. I know you weren't happy when you found out I was keeping company with both whites and coloreds, but dig this: if I'm both races, I should embrace both."

I listen close 'cause she sounds like Ken and Jack.

"I'm not trying to pass for white and fool some honky racists at school. I'm trying to survive. I want to make friends with both sides of my heritage, so I seek out the ones who are OK with that. Those who aren't, well, I don't waste my time on them."

Melissa's hip college views start to make sense to me, and I want us to be real friends, not just brother and sister.

"I didn't mean to get all upset at you," I tell her. "To be honest, I tried to hide my friendship with that black kid on my ball team. I didn't want to admit I really had a colored friend. At least not before I found out *I* was colored—"

I shock myself, hearing those words fall out of my mouth.

"Actually, I like the idea of being a little colored," says Melissa. "Since I do tan so well, the boys at school think I'm prettier than the other girls." She glances down to admire her tanned arms.

I just roll my eyes, and we fall out laughing. I know then that everything will be all right between us. I give her a big hug before she gets up and runs inside. In two minutes she comes back, carrying that dog-eared book of hers.

"Just checked on Mama. She's asleep," she says, fumbling with the pages of the book. "I wanted to show this to you before, but you weren't interested then."

She catches me looking at the pages all bent down on the corners.

"That means the book is worth reading," she says. "This one's about a man named Walter White. He was just like us. A mulatto. See his picture?"

She points to the man on the black and white cover. "In here it says he's got blonde hair and blue eyes."

"But what's so special about him?"

"He became a very important lawyer for the NAACP. And guess what? He's related to President William Henry Harrison."

I can see Melissa's excitement as she shares her book with me. It makes me feel bad we didn't talk about it before. This Walter White person seemed to do OK as a mulatto. It gives me hope that someday I can make a difference and show people that my color won't define who I am or what I can become.

————

I turn fifteen today, but it isn't anything special. Mama gets one of her friends to bake me a cake, and we sit and eat it together. I invited Teeter over to help us celebrate. I haven't seen Mama smile like this in a long time. I'm not sure whether it's that I'm growing up or whether it's because I've finally made friends with someone.

"This is mighty fine cake, Mrs. Lawson." Teeter's licking his fingers and then wiping the little that's left on his napkin. I've been to his house once or twice, too. I don't have too much time to hang out since I'm working and playing ball. But his folks are nice, and we usually play cards or watch TV.

While we eat, Teeter keeps staring at the big yellow envelope that sits on the table in front of us: the Freedom of Choice application. The one that will finally allow me to attend an all-white school. But I missed the deadline again. Now it's sticking out like a sore thumb, just begging for somebody to notice it, even though it's been here a few months now.

"Why haven't you filled this out?" asks Mama, her eyes darting from mine to the envelope.

Teeter keeps his head down and eats real slow, like he's trying not to listen. I've got a mouthful of chocolate cake with extra sweet icing sliding around my tongue. I just shake my head. Mama's eyes widen.

"Why not? You've been waiting for this a long time."

Teeter's eyes dart to mine. Guess he wants to know the answer to that, too.

The cake is going down wrong, so I gulp some milk.

"Stop that," Mama fusses, watching me wipe my mouth with my sleeve. She hands me a paper napkin. "You haven't changed your mind, have you?"

Now she's leaning on her elbows, and a smile is spreading across her face.

I sigh.

"I can't leave Douglass. I mean, I don't want to. I'm doing good in my subjects, and the teachers, well, they really want us to learn."

Teeter sits up a little, and I know he's glad to hear it. I go back to my cake. Mama pats my arm.

"Good. If that's what you want, you stick with it." She gets up and takes her water with her on her way to the living room. "And son," she says, turning around, "Mama's real proud of you."

I smile with tight lips and reach for another piece of cake. Teeter smiles, too.

"After this let's go to your house and watch Batman," I tell him.

We clean up the table and put away the dishes before we leave. I can tell Teeter's used to doing dishes. He's the oldest of four kids, and not one sister among them. When we get outside, we hurry down the stairs, and the sight I see in the parking lot stops me cold.

"What's wrong?" asks Teeter, noticing I'm not in lockstep with him anymore.

"It's that car over there."

I don't dare point; I just motion my head in that direction.

"Nice Mustang," says Teeter. "Whose is it?"

"I'm not sure, but it looks a lot like the one my assistant manager drives."

Teeter resumes walking and waves it off. "Man, there are at least a dozen red Mustangs in town. What, you think he's spying on you or something? No white man got any call being parked over here."

I breathe deep.

"Yeah, you're right. Race you to West Fifth."

Teeter takes off running, and I'm on his heels.

———

It's been a week since the new school year began, and Teeter and I sit in the back of the civics classroom. It really feels like summer has changed things. Not just in me, in the school, too. Not as many people are using chemicals to straighten out their hair. Instead, they're wearing it the way it grows, just natural. They're taking up that Black Power slogan Peter talked about, too. They're dressing differently and say they're doing things like they do them in Africa. When Martin

Luther King died last April, I could see the change coming, just like
Peter said it would.

Teeter taps my shoulder and whispers about the new teacher. "I
heard he carries a gun."

I glance up. It says "Mr. Harrison" on the board. I try to picture him
with a gun in his hand. Most of the teachers around here wear a tie.
Maybe even a jacket, like they're going to church. Not Mr. Harrison.
His hair is thicker than most of the boys in school, and he's wearing a
funny-looking jacket with no lapels and a collar like a preacher. They
call it a Nehru. He's even wearing one of those funny medallions. It's
big, gold, and round with an image on it, but I can't make it out from
here.

Principal Hayes stands at the front of the room with him.

"Thanks to the Elementary and Secondary Education Act passed
last year, we are proud to have Mr. Harrison join our school faculty.
He's a graduate of Howard University in Washington, DC, and has a
master's degree in American history and government."

"I bet he's one of those Snick people, like on the news." Teeter
continues to talk to my back. "I *know* they carry guns."

"So please join me in welcoming Mr. Jimmy Harrison."

Mr. Hayes finishes. We all clap.

"Thank you," says Mr. Harrison. "I'm excited to be here to open
your minds to the inner workings of government, the principles of the
Constitution, and the importance of the Bill of Rights."

Teeter taps me. "Don't he look like a radical to you? That's what I
hear folks calling guys like him. A radical."

Mr. Hayes leaves the room, and we all wait to see what this
strange-dressing, maybe-gun-toting, could-be-radical does next. Mr.
Harrison goes to the blackboard. He picks up the chalk and writes. The
first word he puts up there is ACTIVISM.

Teeter raps me on the shoulder again.

"What'd I say? See?"

I just smile. Teeter is what my mama calls a mess.

Mr. Harrison puts down the chalk, walks to the front of his desk,
and crosses his arms. "Who in here can tell me the definition of this
word?"

He points to Karen, who always sits by the window.

"Activism is standing in a line and marching around to protest something."

Mr. Harrison smiles. "Is that all there is to it?" He points to another kid.

"Isn't it getting involved, like standing up for something you believe in?"

"Now you're on track." He goes to the blackboard. "Activism is the act of using vigorous campaigning to bring about political or social change."

I'm leaning forward now since this new teacher's grabbed my attention. Mr. Harrison comes back to his desk and sits down. He's the first teacher at Douglass who doesn't sit on the edge of the desk. Maybe he's not comfortable yet.

"In this class, we're going to decipher this definition, which means to break it down and examine it piece by piece. In order for you to fully understand the times we are living in, especially here in the South, it's important for you to also understand what it means to be an activist."

He stands and walks between the rows of desks, touching our shoulders, glancing up, and smiling from time to time. He looks my way for a second, and I know I'm standing out like a sore thumb, as usual. He glances away like he doesn't notice my whiteness.

"I want you to imagine you have the ability to live over several decades, say from the 1940s until today. During all that time, you've lived here in the South, and you've been denied all kinds of things: a good job, reasonable housing, and the chance to eat at a nice restaurant. You've even been cursed out almost daily, and maybe even assaulted."

He grasps the edge of a desk in the front of the class and leans forward.

"Tell me, after all you've been through over those decades—never given any respect—and then one day, the folks who have been mistreating you ask you to come live with them. How would you feel?"

Henry raises his hand. He sits in front of me. "I'd say heck no."

Laughter erupts.

Mr. Harrison smiles and nods. "Yes, but *why* do you respond that way? Karen?"

"Well, because if they treated me that way all that long time, why would they treat me any better now?"

"Exactly. You may be wondering what this has to do with activism, and don't forget our definition here," he points to the board. "Many people involved in activism today believe that instituting a vigorous campaign to bring about political or social change is warranted when it comes to integration."

Teeter whispers, "Here it comes."

I'm too busy keeping my eyes and ears tuned to Mr. Harrison to pay him any mind.

"But, keeping in mind our example, when it comes to integration, are they not campaigning, or shall we say *fighting,* for something that is not in the best interest of the people being mistreated?"

The room is quiet, and I figure the rest of the kids are like me, trying to figure that one out. To me it sounds like he's telling us that integration is not a good thing. So I ask him, just in case I'm wrong.

"I thought integration was the solution to segregation?"

Mr. Harrison finally sits on the edge of his desk with his eyebrows pushed together.

"Why would you think that?"

I look around, and everyone has a wrinkled forehead. He asks again.

"Why would integration be the solution? Teeter?"

I smile again. I know whatever Teeter has to say is gonna to be funny.

"I'm not saying this is how I feel about it, but most folks who want integration want to go to the same school or eat at the same place. They want their stuff to be as nice as the other folks' stuff."

My eyes bug out. I can't believe he made sense. I raise my hand behind me so he can give me some skin.

"OK, I can appreciate that," says Mr. Harrison, "but getting back to how we were treated in our example, do you really think these people have changed? Do you really think they are ready to freely share what they have, as if you are suddenly just like they are, after decades of mistreatment?"

Mr. Harrison is on a roll.

"When the man or woman in our example sees signs hung out in public—in public, mind you—that say 'whites only' everywhere and on everything, would that cause feelings of inclusion and acceptance even after such signs are removed?"

We're all quiet now, and Teeter's poking me. I already know what he's going to say. I raise my hand.

"Mark?"

"Well, my Pa always said if people show you who they are, you should believe them. I guess that means that if the folks who mistreated you all of a sudden act like they want to be different, it might not be a good idea to trust them."

Mr. Harrison stands and points at me.

"Good point. Why would you want to be with a group of people you can't trust?"

Mr. Harrison sure has a way of making you think, and that also gets me to thinking about Eddie and me. How I acted one way and then turned out to be another. I wouldn't trust me either.

There's something about this Mr. Harrison. I've never heard a teacher talk like him before, and I'm impressed. Teeter pokes me again.

"I bet he's got a gun right now."

13

*E*very Saturday I get up bright and early to get ready for work so I don't miss the bus. It takes about twenty-five minutes to get downtown, and I don't want to be late. Saturdays are pretty busy because it's the only day working people have time to do their shopping.

"Mark, watch the counter for me," Mr. Miller says as I finish restocking the pickle jar. "I need to go over some numbers with Andy."

I nod as he heads for the back of the store. After a few minutes, no one comes in, so I grab the broom and start sweeping the sidewalk out front. The marchers are back at it again. Their demonstrations are taking place like clockwork every week. Now that I'm downtown more, I can see how organized they are and their determination not to leave, even when some store owners come out and yell at them. They hold up their big white signs with thick black writing.

They walk real slow, back and forth and back and forth. No talking, just walking. At first they would chant, "What do we want? Equality. When do we want it? Now." But the police put a stop to that. They said they were disturbing the peace.

As I watch them, I get confirmation of what I suspected all along. I haven't seen any coloreds come into Mr. Miller's store yet. Not even maids.

I go back inside to see what else Mr. Miller has for me to do when Officer Nick pulls up in his cruiser. He stops in for an orange soda, a dill pickle, and some Turkish Taffy. It's the same every Saturday.

"How's it going, Mark?" He asks me as he picks up the tongs from the counter.

"Great, Nick. Just great." He says to call him Nick instead of Officer Nick. I look past him to his cruiser. "Where's your partner?"

"Gone."

"Why? What happened?"

"He up and quit, you might say. More like he got run off."

I don't ask why. One of the kids at school said his father got on the force and left lickety-split after they harassed him every day. I just pull out a waxed paper bag and get it ready while Nick dips the tongs into the large pickle jar.

"Anything going on today? Any of those folks out there give you any trouble?"

I shake my head while I roll down the top of the bag.

"Good. We don't want them causing any disturbances over here. They're keeping legitimate customers away from these stores. I keep telling Mr. Miller he needs to put a sign in his window like some of the others, claiming his right to refuse customers. You've seen them in some of the storefront windows," he says, pointing the dill pickle outside. "That way none of them Negroes can say anything."

I look up at Nick. "Are you saying Mr. Miller doesn't serve coloreds?'

Nick looks around the store. "Do you see any?'

I shake my head.

"Have you seen any since you've been working here?"

"Well, no."

Nick pulls out a five-dollar bill, lays it on the counter, and opens the cooler to get his orange soda. "So what's that tell you?"

I shrug. He chuckles.

"Miller ain't had no love for coloreds ever since the law allowed them to fight side by side with whites during the war. Him and Andy back there fought to keep them out of the local VFW, too."

Nick picks up the Turkish Taffy.

"But don't you worry about it, son. This stuff'll die down soon, and things will be back to normal; you wait and see." He turns to look out the storefront window. "They'll get enough of protesting as long as the store owners keep resisting."

Just as Nick is about to slap that Turkish Taffy onto the counter, who walks in the store but Becky Gilmore.

SLAM

I jump at the sound.

"What's wrong, Mark?"

Nick opens the wrapper filled with pieces of cracked taffy and pushes it toward me.

"I—I just remembered something I gotta do."

I beg off and immediately run into the storeroom and shut the swinging doors before she sees me. I peek through one of the plastic windows and watch. Mr. Miller's out of his office and talking to Will and Becky.

"Well, he was just here a minute ago," Mr. Miller tattles on me.

I knew it. I knew he was her brother.

"And how do you know Mark?" Mr. Miller asks Becky.

I'm sweating and praying the whole while. She's gonna mess up everything.

"Well, he used to go to my school..."

Oh God, please don't let her ruin this for me.

"Oh really," says Mr. Miller, a little too interested for my comfort.

"Yes," says Becky like she's testifying in court, "but now that he's—

"

"Come on, Becky, I got to get that engine tuned, and Mr. Miller ain't got time to waste on your jabbering."

I let out a sigh of relief as Will drags Becky out the front door.

"Thanks for the advance, Mr. Miller," says Will on his way out. "See you first thing tomorrow."

I come out of the storeroom after I'm sure they're gone. I may have dodged a bullet this time, but what about next time? There's nothing stopping Becky from telling Will. Might be he already knows.

What Nick told me about Mr. Miller took me by surprise. I didn't think he disliked anyone, and though I've never seen a colored person inside these walls, I never heard him say anything bad about coloreds. But I'm not stupid; I had a feeling he might be like most whites in town—at least the ones I know—but once I got here I didn't really want to believe he didn't serve coloreds. What's more important, by the way he's acting, he still doesn't know about me.

I go outside to finish sweeping. The red Mustang is nowhere in sight. I decide to take Nick's advice and quit my worrying. Besides, Mr. Miller likes the work I'm doing, and so far, nothing's happened.

———

I manage to make it through the winter without Mr. Miller figuring out my secret, and with spring on the way, I figure I'm in the clear. Hard to believe it's almost been a year since I was expelled.

None of the white schools have integrated all the way, and no white kids have come to Douglass. Mama says the school system got hit with another court order after they found ways to get around the first one—like building Jeff Davis so small it'd fill up with white kids before coloreds could apply, and pushing for neighborhood schools so colored kids would be forced to stay in colored school districts. She says their mess is liable to go on for years. None of that matters to me anymore because I'm staying at Douglass. I'm not interested in going where I'm not wanted. At Douglass, I'm family.

Mr. Harrison stands at the blackboard, and I know we're in for a treat. He picks up the chalk and writes. The first word he puts up there is CONSCIENCE. He puts down the chalk, walks to the front of his desk, and crosses his arms.

"Who in here can tell me the definition of this word?"

This one is easy, so I give it a try.

"Mark?"

"It means to feel real bad about something you did."

Teeter pushes me from behind like my answer is stupid.

"That's one way to look at it," says Mr. Harrison. He points to Karen.

"It's the thing that bugs you if you do something wrong."

Mr. Harrison smiles, but I look back at Teeter and mouth the words, "Didn't I just say that?"

"But," says Mr. Harrison, with his finger raised to the ceiling, "does it bug *everyone*?"

Wrinkled foreheads fill the room, and that always makes Mr. Harrison happy. He goes back to the blackboard. "The definition of conscience," the hard chalk taps against the blackboard like it's keeping pace with his voice, "is the sense or consciousness of the moral goodness or blameworthiness of one's own conduct, intentions, or character together with a feeling of obligation to do right or be good..."

Mr. Harrison comes back to the desk and sits down. "As you can see in this case, conscience means a lot more than feeling bad about something. Let's break it down. Imagine it's 1954. A black man gets on a city bus, pays his fare, and is expected to get off again so he can re-enter the vehicle using the back door. What do you think the bus driver's conscience is saying?"

I raise my eyebrows in surprise. He's using the word "black" for the first time in class. None of my other teachers use it. He walks past my desk as he goes through the aisles. To my surprise, Teeter isn't tapping my shoulder.

"Teeter?"

"His conscience ain't saying nothing because he don't care about that black man."

"Good answer. Anyone else?"

I turn around and gawk at Teeter. He smiles and nods his head.

"Henry?"

"His conscience could be telling him that what he's making that black man do is wrong, but instead of feeling bad, he's ignoring it."

Mr. Harrison points at Henry like he just won a prize.

"Precisely, Henry. Thank you."

Some of us smirk in Henry's direction. He puts his thumbs under his suspenders like he's a big man.

"Let's go back to our definition of conscience." Mr. Harrison says this as he walks back to the board. He points to his sentence. "Which part of this did the bus driver ignore?"

"Karen?"

"The first part, the sense or consciousness of the moral goodness or blameworthiness of one's own conduct."

"How did the bus driver do the opposite of this? Henry?"

"He didn't have a sense of the blameworthiness of his own conduct."

"But did he have good *intentions*?"

No one says anything. Mr. Harrison smiles again.

"Don't feel stupid over this; I'm not trying to scare you. I'm trying to challenge you. Because, in one way, the bus driver actually thinks he's got a good conscience. Why? Because he's following the law, even though that law is morally wrong."

Mr. Harrison sits on the edge of his desk again.

"I'm going to say it over and over again: Knowledge is power. If you don't know how to shape your thinking to see things from all angles, you're not going to be very good at determining what's really right from what's really wrong. More importantly, to understand how another person thinks. You can never overpower someone's ingrained beliefs or attitudes until you understand how that person came to have them. That's the first step to mental freedom. And *that* is what we will be addressing over the next few days."

He goes behind his desk again and opens a book.

"I want you to take out the books you received today and turn to page fifty-seven."

We all scramble to get the book open. A photo of a white woman stares back at us. One kid after another murmurs and whispers. Henry quickly raises his hand. "Who is Juliette Hampton Morgan?"

Mr. Harrison stands again.

"I'm glad you asked that question, and don't think I didn't notice your faces when you saw her picture there. Yes, she is a white woman, and yes, she was very important to the struggle against racism in this city because she had a good *conscience*. What you'll learn in this class is that part of civics is being a good citizen."

He looks down at the book.

"I'm sure if any of you go home and ask your parents, they may not know about Juliette Hampton Morgan. She became a civil rights activist long before Rosa Parks or Dr. King. This rich, white, long-time southerner did not accept the idea of segregation, and, believe it or not, she did something about it. Let's go back to our example of the black man on the bus. Back in the 40s, when Mrs. Morgan lived, she saw this kind of treatment of blacks every day because she rode the bus—"

"If she was rich, why was she riding the bus?" Teeter blurts.

"Another good question, but next time please raise your hand."

I look back at Teeter and grin. He pushes my head away, and I stifle a laugh.

"Mrs. Hampton Morgan didn't like driving, and it's a good thing too, because she wrote to the local newspaper about the things she saw happening on the bus. It got her into a lot of trouble. But that's not what I want you to focus on. I want you to think about the fact that Mrs. Morgan was white, but she was also rich, which makes a big difference in the attitudes of some whites regarding segregation."

By this time, my eyes are fixed on Mr. Harrison, hanging on his every word, and I'm not the only one.

"Think about it. If you have all the means you need to be successful in life, how much time are you going to spend worrying about competing with someone who's not on your economic level? Most of the white people in this country, Southern whites in particular, are what's called low to middle class. Not the upper-class wealthy. We'll get into those definitions another time. But the point is, those low-to-middle-class whites are competing for the same things low-to-middle-class blacks are competing for."

Henry's hand shoots up.

"Henry?"

"That don't make sense. No colored folks I know can compete with white folks for anything. My daddy can't get no job because the white folks got all the good ones."

"Correction, my young brother. Your daddy can't get that job *yet*, and that is the issue. Segregation guarantees that your daddy can't compete with that white man for the same job. If that white man were rich, he wouldn't need to compete with your daddy. Does it make sense *now*?"

Mr. Harrison is walking around again.

"Now don't get me wrong, there were, and are, plenty of upper-class white politicians and business owners who oppose integration, oftentimes due to the urging of their constituents and customers. To many of them, it's a matter of maintaining their power and economic status."

Mr. Harrison stops at my desk.

"We need to train our minds to realize a few things. First, the civil disobedience Dr. King promoted is not going to make white people who are in the same socioeconomic class as Black folks give up anything on account of their conscience, because it would not benefit them to do so. And second, there are only two things that will assist black folks in putting an end to segregationist practices in the South: rich white sympathizers and pride in our race. Because just like knowledge, black pride is *also* power."

When Mr. Harrison finishes that speech, you can't hear a sound. I never thought I'd say this, but Frederick Douglass High is giving me the best education I've ever had.

14

"Is that all you need, Mrs. Mitchell?" I'm waiting on a few customers because Mr. Miller is in the back with Mr. Anderson again.

"Well, I did want to know when he's going to get in some more of those brown eggs. They taste much better than the white ones, don't you think so?"

I agree with her, even though I've never noticed a difference. Especially after Mama gave me the egg test:

When I turned seven, Mama sat me down at the kitchen table and put two eggs in front of me: one white and one brown. "What's the difference?" she asked with her hands on her hips and an expression that said this answer should be as obvious to me as it is to her.

"One is brown and one is white?"

Mama smiled. She took an egg in each hand and nodded toward the stove. I stood next to her, all of three feet shorter, and watched her crack each one. The sunshine yellow and slimy clear contents fell into the pan and sizzled as they soaked up the surrounding pats of butter.

Mama took the spatula and flipped each one, careful not to break the yolk. She slid them onto one plate and then led me back to the table.

"Here," she said, handing me a fork.

I looked up, and she knew I wanted salt because she sighed and returned to the stove to fetch it. I dug in to one, then the other.

"So?" she said. "Can you tell the difference?"

I shook my head.

"Good. Remember that if someone ever tries to convince you otherwise. The only difference between white eggs and brown eggs is their color."

I nodded and finished my breakfast.

Mama never mentioned the egg test again, until Pa died. At the funeral she sat next to me, and with her eyes fixed on the plain wooden coffin, her trembling lips whispered, "I'm gonna miss my brown egg." I didn't understand what she meant then. I do now.

"Wait here just a minute and I'll ask him," I say to Mrs. Mitchell, putting the last of her items in the big brown bag. "And when I get back, I'll help you put these in your car."

"Such a nice young man."

I walk to the back of the store, where Mr. Anderson makes up the compounds for all our prescription orders. The door is cracked open just enough for me to hear them talking.

"For the hundredth time, Harry, I've got to use the fifty percent potency; otherwise, it may take years for them to feel the effects. You wanted something quick, didn't you?"

"I want whatever works the fastest, so if the Ortho is all you've got, we'll go with that." Mr. Miller sounds angrier than I've ever heard him.

"Did you get those pellets you were supposed to order?" Mr. Miller continues. "We're going to need something that'll fit into the tube of that hose so when we shoot the water at them, it'll run right through."

"Don't worry," Mr. Anderson says, "the Ortho is wettable. It'll mix right in, no problem."

"Once those marchers get a drink of that fire hose, they'll never know what hit 'em," Mr. Miller chuckles.

"Using DDT was a brilliant plan," says Mr. Anderson. "I gotta hand it to you, Harry. You're always thinking."

I step back with my hand over my mouth, not believing what I'm hearing. DDT was a pesticide they used on the farm in Greensboro, and it made Mama's sickness worse than it ever was. The door is opening, so I turn on a dime and walk back to help Mrs. Mitchell.

"Did you want something, son?" I freeze hearing Mr. Miller's voice. I don't know what to do.

Does he know I was listening?

I turn around slowly.

"Uh," I gulp. "Mrs. Mitchell...she wants to know, uh, when we're gonna get in some...brown eggs."

Mr. Miller raises his eyebrow and walks past me toward the front of the store. I look back and see Mr. Anderson slowly close his door.

"Well, Mrs. Mitchell. Find everything you need?" Mr. Miller asks her.

"I surely did with the help of this young gentleman."

"Good, good. Mark's a fine boy," he says, but his eyes don't mirror his words. "We'll be getting more brown eggs on Tuesday. I'll give you a call as soon as they come in."

"Thank you ever so much, Harry." Her smile is all mushy. Mrs. Mitchell does that every time she sees Mr. Miller. She's a widow.

"I'll help you take your bags out, Mrs. Mitch—"

"No need, son. I'll take care of it. You go back to my office and wait there until I get back."

As I watch Mr. Miller and Mrs. Mitchell walk to her car, I wonder if my luck has finally run out. In his office, I sit in the big chair in front of his desk. It feels like I'm melting into it. I can't stop my feet from tapping. There's a mustache of sweat on my upper lip. I wipe it. I see a fireman's coat on the door hook. It says Engine No. 53.

His footsteps get closer, so I sit up. Maybe if I act like nothing's wrong, he won't suspect I was listening, though I doubt it. I'm pretty sure my stammering gave me away. He comes through the door, stands behind his desk for a moment, and then sits.

"Son, you've been working here for some months now, and you do good work. Real good. But there are some things you need to know." He leans over the desk and points a finger at me. "Whenever I'm back here talking to Mr. Anderson, or working alone, or anything, you mind your business, ya hear?"

I perk up. "Yes, sir. Absolutely, sir."

"Now I know you meant well, trying to help Mrs. Mitchell, and that's all right. We have to keep our customers happy. But I'm warning you, boy. You keep your ears up front where they belong and your mouth closed. You got that?"

"Yes, sir. Thank you, sir."

Mr. Miller sits back and rubs his chin. "Now, get out there and keep doing the good job you been doing."

I stand to go. "I sure will, Mr. Miller. I sure will."

I feel like someone put me in front of a firing squad and then changed their mind. I walk out of that office, a weight off my shoulders. Still, it angers me that he plans to hurt people using the same stuff that made Mama's sickness flare up. I know I have to do something, but for the life of me I don't know what.

————

"Stop picking at your dinner." Mama says to me at supper that night. She must be feeling good today. She baked a chicken pie. "You got something working on your mind?"

I look at her, not realizing I've been holding my fork for the longest time and not a bit of food's been on it. I shake my head and shove a helping of pie into my mouth.

Mama's right about something working on my mind. It's deciding whether I should do what's right and find out what Mr. Miller and Mr. Anderson are up to or protect my job. The only job that's bringing money into this house right now. But I can't just ignore my conscience.

"You want to talk about it?" Mama always knows when I'm telling the truth and when I'm not, so I just say no and excuse myself from the table. The last thing she needs is another worry.

In my room, I take my Pa's picture off the dresser and sit with it on the bed. "What am I gonna do, Pa?" I say to him. "What am I gonna do?"

Mr. Miller still thinks I'm white. If he finds out the truth, I'm already a goner. But now it's worse. He's plotting to hurt colored people. If he'd do that to folks he doesn't even know, how much would he punish me?

—————

Before I decide what to do about Mr. Miller, I go back to the library. I need to find out more about that DDT so I can at least get some facts before I make a decision.

I sit at one of the round tables in the main area and scoot my chair close to the window. I could use the extra light, and the sun's bright today. I close my eyes as the heat tingles along my neck and down to my arms like a warm hug. I could sure use one right about now.

I figure since I'm not researching mulattos or any other colored people, I can ask one of the librarians to help me use that card catalog. I look around wishing Ken or Jack was in here to show me again.

"Are you looking for the *definition* of DDT? Because if you are, you can find that in the encyclopedia," says the librarian. She's nicer than the one I met here the last time.

"You mean those books the man comes around and sells at your door?'

"Yes, those are the ones. We have a set here for those who want to read them but can't afford to buy their own."

I remember that encyclopedia man. Soon as Pa saw him coming, he'd run us off the porch and into the house so we wouldn't be talked to death about stuff Pa couldn't explain after the salesman left. I always wanted to see what was inside all those books, but Pa never gave us a chance.

"Here it is," says the librarian as she pages through the big book. "DDT. It stands for dichlorodiphenyltrichloroethane."

We both look at each other like she just read a foreign language that she can't translate.

"I think I'll stick to calling it DDT."

She smiles. "These chemical terms can be pretty tricky. So then, what do you need to know about DDT?"

I scratch my head. I don't want to tell her what I heard, or how I heard it, so I just treat it like homework. "Well, I need to know what it's got in it that makes people sick."

"Hmm, well, it says here that it's approved for use on farms to reduce the number of harmful insects."

"I used to live on a farm, and they used big spray cans full of stuff that looked like mist, but I never knew what was inside. Made my mama sick, though. Does it say anything about how it causes sickness?"

"On the contrary," says the librarian. "According to this, it's been used a lot in foreign countries to eradicate diseases, like malaria."

"What does 'eradicate' mean?" I could use a new word to add to my collection.

"It basically means to get rid of."

"Oh. Like kill, you mean?"

"Well, yes. Kill."

I look over her shoulder at the encyclopedia. "Does it say anything about killing *people*?"

The librarian looks at me with questioning eyes.

"You might be interested in looking over a book we have on the subject. It's called *Silent Spring* and was written by a woman scientist. Very popular book a few years ago. Maybe something in there will help you."

She goes to the shelf to find the book.

"Here it is. Rachel Carson was her name. They showed something on TV about her a few years ago. Maybe you remember seeing it?"

"No, ma'am. We never had a TV back then, and with so much work to do on the farm, we wouldn't a had a chance to watch it."

"It basically said that all pesticides are harmful to human health. From what I remember, lots of people agreed with that." She sets the book on the table. "I've got to check out some other folks, but if there's anything else you need, let me know."

"Thanks," I say.

I flip through the book and find that Mrs. Carson thought scientists needed to be more careful about how they use pesticides, but she never said for sure that they harm people. I know for a fact that it's harmful since it hurt Mama. But if a person doesn't already have an ailment, I guess they wouldn't get sick. No one else on the farm did.

If the stuff is mostly harmless, why would Mr. Miller want to use it on the marchers?

I keep reading until I find that the DDT folks use ranges from five percent to no more than twenty-five percent toxicity. Mr. Miller said something about fifty percent. That would sure be enough to poison people, even if it didn't kill them.

I slump over the books on my table and think. None of this solves my real problem: whether or not I should tell anyone.

I'm racking my brain, but it feels as empty as it did when I came in. Then I get an idea. If I can find the DDT when Mr. Miller's not around, then maybe I can steal it so they can't use it. That way I won't lose my job and the marchers won't get hurt.

Most Saturdays, Mr. Miller is at the store with me, doing inventory or checking out the displays I set up. When he's not, Will takes over. When I get to work Saturday, I'll look at the schedule and see when he's working again. If he is, that'll mean Mr. Miller isn't.

I've been in the storeroom and the freezer before and never saw nothing there that didn't belong. When I lived on the farm, pesticides were kept in a shed with a big red X painted on it, and there's a shed behind the store. As soon as no one's around, I'll take a look.

The next thing I'll have to do is figure out what to do about Will. Teeter told me his daddy looks at girlie magazines, and he gets new ones all the time. If I can get my hands on those, it might just be enough to keep Will busy.

I collect up all the books and take them back to the librarian.

"Find everything you need?"

"Not quite," I say, "but I will, real soon." On my way out I see Ken coming in, the guy I met the first time I came here, from that activist group SNCC.

"Hey Ken."

"Mark. You in here doing another paper?"

I hesitate. I don't want Ken to know what I was doing. "Yeah, it's for, uh, science. Where's Jack? Isn't he with you?"

Ken's eyelids lower. "No, he's not with Snick anymore."

"Why?"

"Well, we got a new leader, Stokely Carmichael. Maybe you've heard of him?"

"A little."

I don't want to say where since I'm not sure what Peter said is reliable.

"Well, now that he's head of the organization, he's focusing more on Black participation, and, well, whites don't feel welcome anymore."

"I heard about him calling for Black Power. Does that mean you guys are violent?"

I needed to ask so I could tell Teeter he's wrong for sure.

"Our message now is that Black people need political power, our own party. We promote that black is beautiful and that being proud of our color is the first step to gaining respect." Ken looks at his watch. "I hate to be rude, but I've got to pick up some books and get back to class. Nice talking to you."

"See ya."

I push through the revolving door and out onto the sidewalk. If more people start to feel like this Carmichael guy, there might not be any integration after all.

As I walk home, I'm not really paying much attention to the street or the folks walking, catching the bus, or shopping, when all of a sudden I get the feeling I'm being watched. I slow my steps and glance over my shoulder long enough to catch a red Mustang a couple blocks back—with white stripes. When it turns down a side street, I shake off the feeling and make my way into the apartment.

———

"For your assignment tomorrow, I want each of you to be ready to explain Darwin's theory. Class dismissed."

I'm sitting in the back of Miss Alice May's class. It's not my period with her, but I asked if I could come towards the end. I want to talk to Eddie after class. She lets me sit in since I have study hall and no homework.

While the students file out, I stay seated, watching Eddie shove his pencil and paper inside his jacket. When he gets up to leave, I stand in his path. "Can you stick around for a minute? I got something to tell you."

Eddie looks back at Miss Alice May. She's real busy, shuffling papers on her desk, but she must've been listening. She gives Eddie a nod.

"I've got to run to the office," she says. "I'll be back to close up the room in about twenty minutes."

After she leaves, we sit. For what seems like ages. Neither of us says a word, but we both feel the uneasiness of the quiet room. Eddie abruptly stands.

"Wait," I plead. "Don't go. I...I really need to talk to you."

Eddie slowly sits himself into the chair. He looks straight ahead, stone-faced as if he doesn't expect to hear anything good.

I lower my lids. "First of all. I'm sorry. I tried to say so that day at your locker, but you wouldn't let me."

I look up to see if his expression changes. It doesn't.

"Eddie, I know I was wrong to shut you out, but I couldn't stand to see you then."

Eddie jumps to his feet. "Because I'm Black, like you? Is that it?"

I stand too, trying to calm him. "No. Not because you're...black..."

With a deep breath, I put my hand on his shoulder. "Because I was stupid, that's why. You were my friend, and I didn't appreciate it."

I turn away. Run my hand through my hair. I can't explain it right, but I want to.

"I was going crazy," I finally say. "Plum crazy. I...just like that, my life was different, and...well...I didn't know what I was doing or saying." I look Eddie in the eye. He returns the stare.

"You're right," he says. "You were stupid. Doggone stupid. You should've told me about it right off. I figured since you didn't, you really weren't my friend. Just another white boy."

I rub my face. "Well, that ain't true anymore, now is it?"

I let out a nervous chuckle.

Eddie's expression turns defiant. "Get real, man. You act like being colored or mixed or whatever you are is some sort of disease. You're still white in your head, Mark. Admit it—".

"What?

"You don't like yourself."

"You're crazy—"

"You don't like being mixed. I used to think you didn't care about color, but I guess that was when you thought you were white. Figures."

"Will you listen to me? I'm not saying a thing against being mixed or colored or anything. What I'm trying to tell you is what happened to me. Can't you understand what happened?"

"Sure I can; you turned black and want me to feel sorry for you—"

"Sorry?"

"That's what I said, sorry. Which is what *you* are—"

"I've been beat up, cussed out, and told off by both coloreds and whites. I lost my race. My race, Eddie. It wasn't fair. I lost my identity, my life—"

"Well, pinch yourself..." Eddie grabs his books. "Then you'll know for sure you're still living."

I exhale hard and stop talking. I slump in the chair with nothing else to say. He swings his gym bag over his shoulder and leaves the room.

I kick the desk where Eddie'd been sitting. This stupid conversation didn't get me anywhere, just like the last one, but I've got to try. Even harder. Because if I don't and he gets hurt, I'll never forgive myself.

15

———————

"**M**an, for half a white boy, you sure don't think like one."

Teeter sits on the desk across from mine, listening to me explain what I saw at Mr. Miller's store. I have to tell somebody, and since Teeter isn't on my baseball team and doesn't go in for all those marches, he's the perfect choice. Plus I need his daddy's girlie magazines.

"How come you stood there and listened? That's what I want to know," said Teeter, still grilling me. "From the time I was knee-high to a dog, my daddy always said, 'If you ever hear something white folks is scheming you get as far away as you can get 'cause sure as you're born they gonna find a way to blame it on you.'"

I shrug, and Teeter's eyes roll back in his head.

"Guess I'm gonna have to do your thinking for you." He says, crossing his arms like the decision's been made. "Now here's what we gonna do—"

Before Teeter can finish, Eddie walks in. He has Mr. Harrison after we do, and his arrival tells us we're already late for our next class. Teeter jumps up, grabs his bag, and nods as he rushes past Eddie. I exchange a stare with my ex-friend, but his eyes don't say anything angry to me. Not like yesterday.

He just looks sad the way kids do when their parents tell them they can't go to the park even though they've been looking forward to it all week. I exchange my cautiousness for a smile and leave before I see his reaction.

———

Teeter and I get back together after school to plan. He thinks my idea to search for the DDT is a good one, so he promises to get the girlie magazines for me.

"Once Will sticks his nose into those pages, he won't be coming up for air for a while," I say, with pride in my voice.

"I still don't think you should do this by yourself. Why don't you let me come along? I can distract that dude in case some customers come in or he gets to wondering where you are and what you're doing."

I rub my chin.

"Besides," Teeter continues, "if old man Miller changes his mind about being off, you'll be in a world of trouble."

"Oh, he's not gonna do that. If he says he's not coming in, he won't come in. I know that much."

"Like I said, for half a white boy, you sure don't think like one. White folks always do the *opposite* of what they tell Black folks. Happens all the time. And I don't care if he knows you colored or not; he ain't gonna leave his store all day to no runt kid and a doofus like Will, if he's as bad as you say."

I sigh deep. I really don't want to hear all this mess from Teeter, mostly because it might be true.

"I just know I gotta get to that DDT. The only way you can help is to be out front watching out. Just stand outside the store like you're waiting on somebody or something. Will ain't gonna let you come in. Mr. Miller don't serve coloreds."

Teeter shakes his head. "Like I said..."

"All right already. Meet me at the store around two o'clock. That's when Will takes his break."

Teeter doesn't respond because he's got his eyes on the side door of the school building. We watch Eddie pause for a moment and walk on down the sidewalk toward West Fifth.

"What's eating him?" Teeter says with his eyes following Eddie. "He acts like he lost his best friend or something."

I watch Eddie too and hope Teeter's right. But before we can be friends again, Eddie's gonna have to shake off what he thinks I'm trying to be and give me a chance to be what I am.

Teeter and I exchange some skin, and then we go our separate ways. If there's one thing I've learned through this whole thing, it's that I've got to stop worrying about what people think. Even Eddie.

———

When Mr. Miller finally takes a day off, we spring our plan into action. At the store, I find Will sitting in the boss's office with his feet on Mr. Miller's desk. I stand in the doorway shaking my head. He pulls them down in a hurry and sits up.

"What is it, kid?"

"Oh, I was just wondering if you might be interested in these." I pull the girlie magazines out of the brown paper bag I'm holding.

"Where'd you get those?"

"Does it matter? Do you want to see them or not?"

A sly smile comes across his face, and he snatches the magazines from my hand.

"You ain't as dumb as you look, boy. Now you get on outta here. Ain't you got work to do?"

I turn to go.

"Leave the bag, just in case."

I leave it. He winks. I wink back.

Everything's all set. I leave Will to his dirty mind and head out the front door. Teeter's hanging off to the side like he doesn't know me. I catch his eye and motion for him to keep an eye out for Will. Then I go around the back.

The shed is set off behind a rickety wooden fence that must have been built before I was born. Its red paint peels off when I touch it. I reach for the rusted lock when Will's voice stops me. I whirl around to see him standing there. Teeter is way back on the sidewalk with the palms of his hands raised.

Now who's not using their brain?

I quickly look at Will again so he doesn't suspect anything.

"Hey, do you mind if I make a copy of some of these?" Will asks.

I let out a sigh.

"Go ahead," I say, and he disappears around the building. I pull the fence behind me. As he goes back around front, I see him push Teeter aside and shoo him away from the store.

I breathe deep, lick my lips, and then unhinge the lock. After I slip through, I close the shed door. Inside there are all kinds of cans for gasoline and other things. I pull the flashlight from my jeans and inspect them. All I need to find is that can that says "Ortho" or "DDT."

A noise. The shed door is moving. I freeze.

"Hey," Teeter whispers. "You find it?"

I motion for him to be quiet and close the door.

"Here it is. Ortho Insect-Be-Gone...50%...wettable...DDT."

This must be it. I look back toward the door and then reach for the rusty, red can. A sudden squeak stops us dead in our tracks. Light fills the shed, enveloping us.

"I'd leave that be if I were you."

I know that voice, and it's not Will's. I turn to see Mr. Miller. Will is just behind him. He looks confused. "Seems your sister was right, Will," says Mr. Miller. "She told me he was nothing but a little nigger."

Will steps closer to me. "Him?"

Mr. Miller's smirk tells me I was wrong about Will. He pats him on the back.

"Your sister came in here a few weeks back looking for you, and that's when I told her I hired a kid she might know. When I said his name, she went white as a sheet."

Will's scratching his head now. "He's colored?"

"I didn't believe it either, so I told her to get me some evidence. I gave her one of them newfangled Polaroids we just got in. Takes instant pictures. Told her to follow him."

Becky? It was Becky's Mustang?

Mr. Miller pulls an envelope out of his apron and holds it up.

"Once I saw these, I knew." He hands the envelope to Will, who sifts through it like it's one of his girlie magazines.

"Wow, I was wondering what she was doing riding all over town the last few weeks. Good thing I got that engine tuned for her."

Teeter's mouth falls open. My eyebrows meet.

It's all making sense now. My daddy always said, "There's two things in this world that can bring a man to ruin: a bad reputation and a vengeful woman."

"Funny I never asked where you lived on the Southside," Mr. Miller continues, taking the photos back from Will. "Thanks to Becky, I know the truth."

I'm sweating bullets now. Teeter stands closer to me as if I can protect us both.

"She saw you walking down Carter Hill and going into those colored apartments. You're nothin' more than a nigger trying to pass for white. I'll be damned." The look on Mr. Miller's face makes my cheeks burn. "After that bit of news, I figured you'd do something stupid. Now look at you. Trying to stick your nose in where it ain't wanted. I'm very disappointed in you, son, after all I've done for you and your mama. Took you in like you was my own, and now I find out you ain't nothing but scum."

He steps over to a group of belts hanging by hooks on the shed wall. He reaches for something. It's a long, leather whip. I step closer to Teeter. Our arms touch, sharing each other's sweat.

"But there's nothing you can do about my plan, boy. I'm gonna make sure that not a one of them darky heifers at that march ever brings another pickaninny like him into this world."

He points to Teeter. I back away until I bump into a sawhorse. I grab hold of it as if that's gonna save me from this racist bent on keeping us quiet.

Mr. Miller's admiring the whip, like Mama would look at a new teacup. "When I was your age, my daddy gave me this," Mr. Miller says, running it along the palm of his hand until the end falls to the ground.

My lips tremble, but I don't say a word. Teeter's eyes glaze with fear. We both know what's coming. I glance around the shed for an escape.

Mr. Miller laughs at me. "When I get done with you two, you'll know better than to try and fool a white man."

Mr. Miller spreads his legs wide and cracks the whip against the ground at his side. Dirt leaps into the air. I flinch. "Do you know that I got so good at using this whip, I could swat a gnat off my horse's ear without rousing him?"

"Don't do this, Mr. Miller. "Don't," I say. "At least let him go." I nod to Teeter.

Mr. Miller ignores me. He turns to Will.

"Go back to the store. Close the door behind you."

My whole body trembles, and the heat of my shame rises. My groveling only makes him smile. My mind recalls what Mama said about racists taking your self-respect. I won't let him take mine.

Quick as I can, I dive for Mr. Miller's legs like I'm sliding to second base. I knock him down, and the tail of the whip flies up. He falls against the shed door, which busts down, bathing us in sunlight. Teeter grabs the DDT by the handle and jumps over Mr. Miller.

"Run, Teeter! Run!"

Teeter hikes himself over the fence next door, and he's gone. Will rushes back.

I scramble to my feet, but he trips me. Mr. Miller is cursing as he gets himself up. I hear the rushing of that whip before I feel it.

CRACK

I fall to the ground. A shooting sensation like burning hot coals runs up my back. Before I can move, he swings the long piece of leather high and wide.

CRACK

The pain laps across my back like lightning, and I stumble away from the shed toward the store. Will grabs me from behind, making the sting of my wounds even worse. He pulls me around to face Mr. Miller, so I use the only weapon I have left.

"Shit, the damn fool bit me!"

I pull free of Will and stumble away. Mrs. Mitchell's voice floats around the corner. She must be out front.

"Somebody's coming," Will warns.

He grabs Mr. Miller's arm and pulls him away.

I run as fast as my pain will carry me, past some man standing on the side of the building looking at us. I keep running. I don't know what happened after that. It's all flashes. I collapse into a barbershop parking lot. My eyes close and open. Teeter is standing there.

Two arms pull me. I'm in and out of consciousness. I fall to my knees. My back burns, and when I touch my shirt, flesh sticks to it.

"Oh God. Oh God."

"Hush up now, it's gonna be all right," Teeter reassures me. "These men are gonna help."

"Glory be, son, what happened to you?" One man's face gnarls, and his wild eyes dart back and forth. "We gotta get you to a hospital."

"No, please. Just a wet rag or something... please. I...I can fix it."

Teeter glares at me. "You crazy? You need a doctor."

"You done been whipped, son," says the man. "I ain't never seen no white boy whipped like this here—"

"I'm not white." I say between the stings of pain. "I'm Black...like you."

They look to Teeter, and he nods.

"What's going on?" Another man comes over. They seem to know each other.

"Lloyd, come on, man. We gotta get this boy to a hospital, but he don't wanna go."

The other man shakes his head. "You don't want to get involved in no white boy whipping."

"He ain't white," Teeter adds.

"He says he ain't white, Lloyd. Now we got to *do* something."

The two men get on either side and lift me up.

"Owww."

"Easy, son. Easy. We gotta get you into the car."

The men drive me and Teeter to Professional Center, the hospital for colored people, and they take me inside.

"He done been whipped," says the first man who found me.

"I can see that," says the nurse, her eyes full of doubt.

"Oh no, we ain't had nothing to do with it," says the first man.

"Sho' didn't. We found him in the parking lot over at Sly's Barbershop. Says he lives in Eastman Apartments."

"A white boy? Living in Eastman?" The nurse crosses her arms.

Teeter's face disagrees. "He ain't white."

"You got to *do* something," the man pleads.

The nurse pulls up my shirt. The cotton shreds pull away from my skin, and I scream.

"I'm sorry, but I've got to take a look," she says.

The two men look, too. Teeter's mouth falls open.

"You guys get on out of here. I'll take it from here."

"Yes, ma'am. Come on, Lloyd," says the first man. He waves at me. I lift my hand a little to wave back, but it hurts.

"I'm staying," Teeter says with defiance.

"Thank you," I whisper.

"Come on, son, I'll get the doctor to see you right away."

I hesitate, and the nurse knows I want Teeter to stay with me, but she refuses.

"I'll be outside," he says.

While I'm at the hospital, the doctor asks to contact my mother, saying he can't treat me any further than cleaning and bandaging my welts. I refuse. Instead, I take what I can get. I can't let Mama know what's happened. It would break her heart that I've lost my job, but more than that, I don't want her to see my back.

"I could report this to the authorities," the doctor says, but I shake my head.

"Like I told you, it was just a kid fight. There's nothing to tell."

He rubs his chin, and I know he doesn't believe me, but I don't care. If this gets reported, the police won't do anything anyway.

The nurse comes back in. The doctor's eyes shift from me to her. He nods and leaves. The nurse leaves too, but just for a minute. When she comes back, she has her purse, and she pulls out some change.

"Here," she says, handing me a few dollars. "Be careful not to sit back on the ride home."

She smiles, and that puts me at ease.

Once outside I find Teeter on one of those cement benches. He jumps when he sees me. "Man, what'd they let you go for? They call your Ma?"

"No," I say, limping past him. I'll tell her when I get home."

Teeter supports my elbow as we board the next bus. The whole ride I'm sitting straight up so I don't lean on my back.

"I think the bandages make it worse," I say to Teeter. He just shakes his head like I'm a danged fool. The pain hurts something awful, so I hold tight to the front rail each time the bus jolts forward.

At Teeter's stop I wave him away. "Go on, I'll be OK."

I can tell he's disappointed as he hops off the last step. Once I get in the house, I go straight to my room.

"Mark?" Mama calls, but I can't talk to her now.

I shut the door and go to the mirror. I see scratches and welts on my arms and neck. I don't know how I'm going to explain them. The pain stabs me as I dig through my drawer to find a long-sleeved shirt, one with buttons so I don't have to pull it over my head. I don't think I could manage that if I tried.

I head downstairs to tell her that I'm OK. She meets me at the bottom. Her face is worn like she's been crying.

"The hospital called," she says.

I lower my head, and she leads me to the living room, being careful not to touch my back.

Why did I tell the doctor her name?

"Are you going to tell me who did this?"

I don't speak. If I say it was a fight, she'll want to know which kid so she can call their parents. If I say Mr. Miller, the story will get all turned around, and I'll still get blamed.

Mama's mouth is tight, like she's holding back spit. She stands and faces me. "You were at work when this happened?"

I let out a long breath. Mama knows my schedule, and she also knows I wouldn't miss a day of work for anything. But I still keep silent.

"If Mr. Miller whipped you, Mark, keeping it a secret is not going to put him in jail where he belongs."

My eyes widen. "It was like I told the doctor—"

"I don't care what you told the doctor, Mark, I'm not stupid. I know an adult did this. So either you tell me who or I'll go down to Miller's Grocery and—"

"And what, Mama? You think he's just gonna confess to it? You think he's gonna admit he did this? No, if you go down there, it's just gonna make things worse. Nobody cares if a colored boy gets whipped. Nobody."

Mama sits and puts her head in her hands. She's not doing so well today, and I don't want her to worry, so I decide not to tell her what I plan to do.

"Mama, I'm sorry, and you're right. I stuck my two cents in where it wasn't wanted, and he whipped me. But I'm not gonna retaliate 'cause it won't do no good. Don't you go worrying about me; I won't go getting myself in any more trouble. When this is all healed, I'm gonna just let it be."

"Promise your Mama."

I don't know what it is, but there's something different in Mama's eyes as she looks at me, like she's searching for something. Not in an accusing sort of way, but in a sad way, like folks look when they're going away for a real long time and they're telling you how much they're gonna miss you just with their eyes.

She takes my hands in hers and squeezes. I squeeze back. "Your mama loves you, you know that, don't you?"

My brows knit together. "Yes, ma'am."

"You be a good boy, Mark, and always remember what me and your daddy taught you about life and love and God."

"Mama, is everything all right?"

"As long as you promise your mama, everything's gonna be just fine."

"I promise."

16

———————

The next morning Mama opens my bedroom door.

"Someone's here to see you," she says. "It's Teeter. Says he wants to give you something."

I wince trying to get up too fast.

"I can tell him to come back when you're feeling better," she says, about to close the door.

"No. No, I want to see him."

I sit up some when he walks in. He smiles. So do I.

"Glad to see you're in one piece," he says.

I motion for him to sit on the stool next to the window. He does.

"It's in a safe place. The container, I mean."

That news makes me feel a lot better.

"Good thing you're not half a white boy, or else you might not have thought to grab it," I say.

"Ahh, you know what I meant. You just take too many chances. Don't use your head," he says, poking his Afro. "Now how you plan to use that container to finger Mr. Miller? Who's gonna believe it came from his shed? Or even that he's gonna use it on anybody?"

I sit back real careful and let out a long breath because I still haven't come up with the answers.

"Well, you just hold on to it. I'll figure something out after I get well."

Teeter stands. "OK, but before you go sticking your nose in somebody else's business, do me a favor?"

"What?"

"Don't."

I smile and wave him out of my room. "Teeter? Before you go, I just want to say, thanks. Thanks for being there."

"Trust me, the next time you do something foolish like that, I won't be." He raises his fist at me and then closes the door behind him.

———

After my wounds heal a bit, I get back to school. I don't dare tell anyone what happened, though their eyes are asking tons of questions. No one can see my back, but no matter how many times I changed my clothes this morning, I couldn't find a shirt that covered everything. The scabs are tight and itchy. Teeter brought some Vaseline and helped me put it on in the bathroom between classes.

I've got to heal up quick. With baseball season starting soon, I need to be in tiptop shape so I can take whatever the Bloodhounds dish out. They'll be gunning for us this year on account of our beating them in Greensboro.

I'm sitting in Mr. Jordan's history class trying to avoid the kids' stares and keeping my back straight as a board. Everyone is still talking after the bell, and Mr. Jordan isn't saying anything. Most times he doesn't miss a trick, but right now his face is down and his brows are up. He's reading something.

I look down too, inside my history book, which is pretty hard to do with a straight back. I can feel the eyes on me. Mr. Jordan stands and brings the thing he was reading around to the front of his desk.

"All the teachers," he says with a low voice, "received a memo in our boxes today." He stops talking and sits on the edge of his desk. He rubs his forehead with the back of the hand that holds the paper. Something is wrong. "Now, I know some of you have friends or cousins attending Drew High, so I wanted to make sure you heard what happened before you got home because they'll likely be talking about it on the local news."

Now he's got everyone's attention.

I look around the room. Sometimes when stuff happens, a few of the kids in class already know about it. But by the looks on their faces, they're just as in the dark as I am.

"Authorities found the bodies of two adult black males...and one, teen male...buried outside Hale County, in an area where the new dam is under construction—"

Gasps go up, and my heart pounds because Hale County is Greensboro.

"The identities of the two men are still under investigation, but they know for sure that the teenager is fifteen-year-old Peter Jackson."

My head drops to the desk, rousing the pain in my back. I wince. My face tingles and my nose runs. I hold back tears. From the reactions on their faces, only a few kids knew Peter.

"Are you okay, Mark?" asks Mr. Jordan. He touches my shoulder, and I grimace. His eyes question me, but it doesn't last. I look around, and the kids still stare.

"Yes, sir," I sniff. "He was on my baseball team. He helped us win the championship last year."

"Well, I'm sorry to have to tell you what happened." He walks back to his desk. "Let's all bow our heads and say a silent prayer for Peter, his family, and the two men."

Mr. Jordan lowers his head. The rest of the kids do too, so I join in. While our eyes are shut, I say in my head, *"How could God let something like this happen?"* Though I know Peter wasn't the nicest kid, he didn't deserve to die.

But Mama says God doesn't hate, so I talk to the Devil instead. *You're gonna get yours one day,* I say silently, *just like Mr. Miller. You're gonna get yours, and everybody on Earth is gonna to cheer loud and long.*

———

Peter's funeral is at a small church not far from the apartment, so I walk down Carter Hill in my cut-down suit. I've not worn it since the dinner at Billy's, so Mama had to let down the legs too. No chance of seeing the Justices there, so I don't worry about it. I saved up some money from my job, so I got a new pair of shoes from the Salvation Army. At least now my toes aren't cramped. I wiggle them inside my white socks as I walk.

I see lots of cars in the parking lot of the church, and a black hearse sits right out front. The men getting out of the car wear black, too. My heart sinks. People should wear white to funerals to make them happy.

I walk slow. I'm not in a hurry to see death. I mean, I want to pay my respects like Mama said, but I don't know if I can take it. Seeing him in a casket and all. Mama says if he looks bad, they won't open it. I don't even want to think about what he looks like.

Inside the church the air is suffocating. I pull at the collar of my white shirt. There's a lot of people in here, so I look around for a wall so I can stand out of the way. I still can't lean against nothing since my back's not completely healed, so I keep my hands behind me to hold me away from it. I watch and wait. I see Eddie coming in with his mother. He doesn't see me, for the crowd.

Women whimper as they shuffle past. Every once in a while someone cries out, and I flinch. This whole thing is a drag, and I want to go home.

"How you doing, son?"

The voice rattles me. It's Coach Collier.

I wipe my forehead.

"I guess I'm OK, sir. I-I don't like funerals."

"Me neither."

Coach raises his hand toward the entranceway and waves. Eddie notices us and makes his way over. I know he's coming for Coach, not me. I lower my head and keep my hands behind my back, trying to look away as he gets close.

"Glad you could make it, Eddie," says Coach.

"Yes, sir," says Eddie in a quiet voice.

I look over at him, and he forces a smile. The least he can do is be friendly.

I came, didn't I?

None of the other guys did, at least not that I can see. Guess he's gonna punish me forever. Still, I hope he doesn't go to that march Saturday. I sure hope he doesn't.

"Thanks," comes out of his mouth, and I'm not sure he's even talking to me. Then he puts a hand on my arm. "For Peter, I mean."

"Sure," I say, feeling like a heel. Here I am fussing about *my* feelings when a kid is dead. A kid we both knew. A kid who had lots of talent.

"We better go on in," says Coach Collier.

"I gotta go sit with my mom."

"Say hello to your mother for me when you get back over there," says Coach.

Eddie leaves us before I can say anything else. I hope I can get him to listen to me before the march.

Coach and me walk down one of the sloped aisles with rows of chairs on either side. The dull, red carpet tells the story of too many years of prayer marches, weddings, and funerals. I can't breathe in without getting a nose full of strong perfume from the flowers and old women.

We sit in the back by a window. A thud gets my attention, and soon the grey metal air conditioning unit blows air at my head. I close my eyes and feel it brush against my skin. It's the only pleasant thing going on in here.

"I don't see any of the other boys, do you?" asks Coach, like he's counting heads for the roster. "It'd be nice if a few of 'em showed up."

Yeah. It'd be nice but not likely.

The whine of the organ sounds like the one at Mama's church, but the tune is slow and deliberate. My eyes survey the crowd of people as they look for friends, settle rowdy children, or share a hug and a tissue. Way on the other side is Eddie and his mother. He's got his arm around her. I sigh and decide that I'll just deal with this until it's over. If he can take it, so can I.

———

The usual stuff happens. The preacher gives a sermon about how sad it is to lose another young Negro boy, people fan themselves as the line of mourners shuffle past the casket, and women wail and whimper. I don't get in the line. Neither does Coach. We sit and allow the others to go by.

When the line gets to Eddie's row and he and his mother get up, I lower my head. I don't want him to shame me with that "why aren't you up here" look. After everyone files past the casket, the preacher comes back to the pulpit.

"We all know how hard Dr. King and others are working to free us from the oppression and injustice we've suffered all these years at the hands of the white devil. But today is not a day to celebrate hate. Today is a day to celebrate hope..."

"Amen" rises from the crowd. But not just Amen. A man in the front row abruptly stands and shouts.

"Naw. This ain't no day of hope. Hope? What hope have we got against the Klan and the police..."

People shift in their seats, and some support him, yelling, "Tell it!" and "Preach!"

"Please be seated," says the preacher, "this is a church of God—"

"Then where is he? Where is God when our kids are gunned down or beaten?" asks the man. "We don't need hope; we need action. We need Black Power to stop all this foolishness. Just like Stokely says."

People jump from their seats and clap. The preacher comes down from the pulpit and wraps his arm around the man. He cries. It's Peter's father. The organ swells, and the choir sings a soft, slow song.

The funeral lasts two hours, which is an hour too long in this hot suit. Coach and me take baby steps behind all the people making their way to the exits at the same time. I look up at the backs of heads and then down to my shoes to see if we're getting anywhere.

The next time I look up, I see the back of some light brown hair. I know that head, and I nudge Coach.

"Isn't that...Winston?"

Coach strains to look.

"Sure is." He smiles at me. "Doggone if he didn't show."

Once we get outside, Coach grabs him by the arm.

"Oh, hey, Coach."

When Winston sees me, he just nods.

"Who'd you come with, son?"

Winston points to the street where Billy and Coach Justice stand by their car. Bosley's there too, and I hope he's not decided to take up with Billy. "They didn't want to come in, so they sent me."

I take a deep breath. Billy's only here to make sure Peter's good and dead. Coach Collier must be reading my mind.

"You know why he's here, don't you?" I give Coach a smirk but keep my thoughts to myself. "Matt's coming home from the war. His arm was blown off during a raid—"

"What's that got to do with Peter?" I ask, confused.

"A colored soldier saved his life," says Coach.

I look over at Billy. He's not smiling at all, but I don't allow myself to feel sorry for him. All he's got is guilt, and he should.

I shake Coach's hand. "I'm going to go now."

"OK, son. And thanks for being a man and paying your respects to Peter."

I look at him funny. "Why wouldn't I come? I'm black too, you know."

He nods, and I head for home.

17

A few days before the march, I walk onto the ball field for the first practice of the season, knowing two things. One: I have to find a way to make Eddie listen to me. Two: I need to stop Mr. Miller from hosing the marchers Saturday. Trouble is, I have no idea how to do either one.

At the batters cage I grab my Louisville Slugger, keeping an eye out for Eddie with each swing. After my arm limbers up, I take my seat on the bench, pick up some neatsfoot, and oil my glove. That's when I get an idea. Most of the guys are here, and since the coaches are in a huddle, I know this is as good a time as any.

"Hey guys," I say. "Come over here. I got something I need to tell you."

One by one, they lay down their bats or drop their balls and gather around me near the fence. Eddie comes too, though a lot slower. He lingers behind the rest like he's really not interested.

"I've got something to tell you, and I hope after I do, you'll want to do something about it, like I do." I stand before them as determined as I can be, shaking like a leaf. But I have their attention now, and I can't back down.

"What is it?" asks Bosley.

"Yeah, what's so important?" Hank whines.

I rub the sweat from my face real quick and just blurt it out. "There's gonna be a colored march on Saturday, and well, my boss, Mr. Miller, is a member of the volunteer fire department, and they're planning to put poison in their hoses. They're gonna turn them on the marchers."

At first, the guys don't say anything. My eyes search theirs for a reaction but get none. I know Eddie heard.

Billy Justice pushes his way through to me. "What do we care what happens to them niggers? Let 'em get hosed. It'll teach them a lesson."

My insides feel like a red-hot furnace. "Guess Peter's funeral was a big joke to you." I respond. "There's been enough violence already, and for what? Because of somebody's color—"

"Peter got what he deserved," Billy scoffs. "Him and his rowdy friends beat up a lot of white people after the championship, so I'm not feeling sorry for him at all."

"What kind of poison?" Winston steps between Billy and me. "And how do you know the hoses got poison in them?"

"It's DDT," I say. "I saw the stuff and everything. And when I found out what he was planning, my boss took the whip to me."

I turn around and pull up my jersey. I can hear gasps and other noises over my shoulder. Some of the boys' mouths fall open. Eddie just stands back and stares.

Billy swings his hand in the air. "You gonna believe him? He's colored, so of course he's gonna say that." He comes closer to inspect my back. "I bet you did this yourself, just to get attention. That Mr. Miller's probably a good guy, and you're just accusing him because he's white, like you niggers do."

I pull down my shirt and face Billy. "That's what you think. You don't know him. Besides, how could I do this to myself?" I turn to the others, hoping they believe me. I try hard to keep a stern expression. I have to persuade them to see my side. "If we don't do something to stop him, more people are gonna to get hurt."

"Only colored people. Who cares?" Billy starts to walk away, waving to the others to join him. "Come on, you guys. Let's play ball."

"What do you expect us to do, Mark?" asks Bosley, who seems at least a little interested.

"I'm going to that march on Saturday," I say, "and I ain't gonna let them hose those marchers. If you got anything good in you, you'll do the same."

"That's enough of all this talk," says Coach Justice, who walks up to us. "Nobody is going to march, you hear me? You stay away from them things. Now get in position."

"What's going on here?" Coach Collier's hands are on his hips. His I-mean-business stance.

"Nothing," says Coach Justice. "Everything's fine, right, boys?"

The guys nod, get back to their spots on the field, and we finish our practice. Eddie keeps looking at me. He never says anything. I didn't plan to tell as much as I did, but the idea seemed right at the time. Now at least it's out in the open.

I figure there's no sense in me staying around since I can't get them to cooperate.

I start for home when someone runs up behind me. I figure it's Eddie, but when I turn around a white face stands in front of me.

"Lawson—wait a minute." The last person I expect is Billy Justice. "What *was* that back there?" he asks me, his face as hard as cement.

"Don't talk to me." I say, returning his stone-faced stare. "You got me arrested, and I went to jail because of you."

But when I turn to go, he grabs hold of my arm. "I didn't tell my dad not to hire you. Honest, I didn't."

"You're a liar."

I want to spit on him, but I know that won't solve anything. I need to be better than that, like Miss Alice May says.

"Everybody don't have to know you're colored," he says, softening his expression. "I mean, hell, your mom's white, and your daddy couldn't have been that dark."

"What do you care?"

I continue walking, and he grabs me again, this time with both hands.

"You're throwing away your whole life taking on this colored thing when you could do better."

I yank my arms from his grasp. I can't believe what I'm hearing.

"Look, Lawson, I'm offering you a chance to come back to the right side. The winning side. I'll even get my dad to change his mind about that job. Whaddya say?"

I hesitate. I have to admit that a part of me wants everything he says: to get a job again so I can help Mama. To be respected and treated fairly. I stand there staring at him, and the only words that I can get to come out of my mouth are "Get lost."

I resume my walk home, but he keeps calling out to me.

"All right, go ahead. Go ahead and throw your life away. You belong with that worthless trash."

A twinge starts deep down inside me, and it grows real fast. So fast it turns into a thunderous wave and rushes through me. It makes me turn on my heel and stomp right up to his face.

"Look here, Justice, I've had it with you. You're so stupid you don't even know you're stupid. I thought you'd be different after that black soldier saved Matt—"

Billy's face turns pale.

"That's right, I know about it. But I guess I was stupid too, thinking anything a black person did for you would be enough. You're so burnt up with hating you can't even see straight."

"You don't know—"

"Oh yes, I do. You don't even treat your own maid with respect, so how in the world could I expect you to show it to anyone else?"

"You're just a white nigger—"

"And you're a damn idiot. Name-calling is all you know how to do, and that's just what I'd expect you to say because you can't even defend your stupid hate."

He smirks like he's not listening, which only makes me angrier. So I grab his arms and force him to pay me attention.

"If I could, I'd snatch that blotchy skin clean off your face so you could see you got the same bones as me, as Eddie, or as anybody else. You're ugly to the bone, Billy, and when it all comes off on your dying day, nobody's gonna care 'cause you'll be deader than a doornail, and good riddance to ya!"

I sense power growing inside me for finally standing up to him.

Then Billy does something that catches me off guard. He snatches himself away and steps back. He's reaching into his back pocket, and my eyes grow three sizes.

I lunge for the baseball card, but Billy holds it high and away.

"Give me back my Mantle."

Next thing I know, he's running backwards. He's grabbing the card with both hands. As if in slow motion, my arms reach out to save all the tiny, jagged pieces of Mickey Mantle's face as they float to the ground. My heart is in my throat. I fall to my knees, crawling from spot to spot, snatching after scraps of my pa's card, and stuffing them in my pocket.

Booming laughter brings me to my feet.

Billy's fast, but he can't outrun me. I pounce on his back and knock him to the ground. I punch and kick and punch and kick until somebody pulls me off him.

"What you trying to do, kill 'em?"

"Yes," I say, panting hard and heavy. "I want to kill 'im."

Coach Collier isn't as strong as I thought. I could get away from him easy, but I don't.

Coach Justice runs up and takes hold of his son's bloody shirt. "You're gonna pay for this."

I already have, still staring with blurry eyes at the scraps left on the ground.

Coach Collier finally lets go.

"Go home and clean yourself up, son. You look awful."

Coach Justice drags Billy away, who keeps looking back at me screaming. "You nigger...NIGGER."

For some reason it makes me walk taller every time he calls me that. And as I walk, his words drift further and further away, and so does my desire to ever be anything like him.

―――――

On the day of the march, I run into the bathroom and throw some water on my face. I still don't have a plan for what I'm going to do once I get to the march. I wipe my hands on the white linen towel

Mama left hanging on a hook behind the door.

Before I leave, I check on her. She's asleep. Lying there so peaceful. I tiptoe to the bed and slowly lower my head to hers. I kiss her cheek, and something strange comes over me, a chill I can't explain. I rise up, and it's gone. I close her door and head out.

Walking down to Water Street, I'm more aware of my heartbeat than I've ever been in my life. I steady my breathing so I don't run out of energy. I'll need all I can muster if something goes wrong. I jump from one thought to another—my first day at Douglass, Eddie screaming at me the day I came back to practice as a colored boy, Billy's angry words ringing in my ears.

I shake my head to force myself to think of something good. I even second-guess my determination to stop Mr. Miller. Deep inside I'm shaking like a leaf, but I know that no one else cares about what happens to those people if they get hosed with poison today.

Why do *I* care so much? Billy was right. I can be white if I go somewhere nobody knows me, just like Johnny Mack. But the fact is, I'm not, and I know it. Even if no one else does.

Lord knows what my father's life must have been like as a man looking white and being colored. I never knew the things he suffered, and I guess he never wanted me to know. And Mama, loving a man who looks like her but still isn't like her. It hurts me to imagine what she had to listen to from neighbors and even her family. I never knew about that either, and now that I have to live that same life—stuck between two groups that mostly hate each other—I understand.

Coming up Water Street, I see the marchers in a line on the sidewalk catty-corner from the train station. I see women and men, even a few young people, holding up signs.

EQUAL OPPORTUNITY AND HUMAN DIGNITY
SEGREGATION IS MORALLY WRONG
END SEGREGATED RULES IN PUBLIC SCHOOLS

At first, I stand at a distance. I don't see anyone else besides the protesters. No one is doing anything unusual. On the opposite side of the street, from where the marchers stand, a few white people yell at them as they go about their shopping. I squint into the group to see if any of those young people in line look like Eddie.

They continually walk from one end of the block and return. They hold their signs at a steady height or bob them up and down. As they come around the second time, I see him. He's the third from the end with his hands tightly wrapped around a sign about the schools.

I walk across the street toward him. I don't know what I'll say, but I keep going until I walk right alongside him.

He hesitates when our eyes meet, but only for a moment, then he keeps walking, like he's decided that quick to ignore me. But I stick to him.

"Eddie," I say, trying to talk and walk a straight line. "I came here to warn you about the firemen."

"I don't need you to warn me about nothing," he says, still looking straight ahead. "This is a peaceful march, and ain't nobody gonna bring out no hoses." He bites his lip as he walks, like he's hiding the fact that he's worried. That tells me that at least he heard.

"I wouldn't be here if this wasn't something serious," I say, half watching where I walk. Every now and then I slip off the curb and have to catch my balance.

"Why don't you just leave us be, before some white folks come over here thinking we're bothering you?"

Right then I step out of line and do what he asks. He's right. A few of the people across the street egg me on, like they think I'm on their side.

The sun is warm, even though the wind feels cool. I look up and down the street again, thinking that maybe I'm wrong. Maybe there won't be any hosing, and I should go back home. Then I see Teeter coming down the street. He's carrying a big shopping bag. We exchange glances, and he nods toward the bag. A feeling of relief washes over me. Now, if something happens, I've got proof.

I start across the street. There's a siren. My head turns in that direction. Around the corner comes a red fire truck with No. 53 painted in gold on the side—the same number Mr. Miller has on his volunteer fireman uniform. I step back onto the sidewalk to avoid the truck, which is followed by two police cars and an emergency vehicle.

My palms sweat as I watch them pull up close to the marchers. Mr.

Miller and another fireman climb down from the truck wearing their fire coats. The second man is Mr. Anderson.

The policemen step out of their cars and approach the picket line. "Do any of you all have a permit to demonstrate in front of this here establishment?"

No one says a word. They just walk slow and deliberate.

The officer repeats his question. Again, no response.

I want to run right over to him and tell him what the firemen are planning and what I know, but something makes me hold back. I need to see them go for the hoses first. I need to make sure I'm right.

One of the officers goes back to his squad car and pulls out the hand radio. While he talks on it, the other officer stays with the marchers. He has his nightstick out and taps it into the palm of his left hand. He approaches the marchers and asks them to disperse. They don't, and he calls a few other officers to come over. They pull out their nightsticks too and poke the protesters with them like they're rounding up cattle. But the marchers don't resist; they just get pushed back, back, back. A few of them get pushed so hard they fall to the ground. When others come to help them, the cops kick them and push them back. All the while, the marchers just won't go.

A crowd of white people gathers closer to the sidewalk, but far enough not to get in the way. They watch like it's a sports event. It sickens me how they smile, laugh, and jeer at the marchers.

I take my eyes off them long enough to notice Mr. Miller unrolling the fire hose.

No, this can't happen.

I don't even know when my feet start to move, but I find myself walking quickly toward the red fire truck. Next thing I know, I'm running right up to Mr. Miller.

"Don't do this." I beg with tears glazing my eyes. "Don't do it."

I feel someone grab my arms and pull me out of the way. It's another officer. It's Nick.

"You gotta stop him," I scream. "He's gonna kill them."

I struggle to get out of his grip, but he drags me toward the car. I scream louder, and some of the crowd comes toward us, not knowing that I'm colored. They actually plead with Nick to let me go.

Then Mr. Miller says, "He ain't one of us. He's a nigger just like them." And the two people who offered me help look confused.

Nick still holds me. "Mark, we have to leave now."

He puts me in the police cruiser but doesn't handcuff me, just sticks me in the back seat. I turn to the back window and watch helplessly as the scene gets further away from me, along with my ability to do anything to stop this horrible crime.

My eyes blur, and then I see something amazing. Two boys are walking in front of the fire truck. No, it's more than two.

"Stop, stop the car," I yell at Nick. "Please, I have to get out."

"I'm sorry, son, we have to take you to the hospital." I turn away from the window in confusion. But I ignore what he says. "Please, let me out. My team is back there."

I can't believe it when Nick stops the cruiser. I jump out and run to the march. Standing there, between the marchers and Mr. Miller's fire hose, is most of my ball club. Bosley is leading them. They're forming a human chain.

My eyes are too glazed to see very well, but I run right up to them and join in, taking Winston's hand. He starts chanting:

NO, NO, WE WON'T GO

NO, NO, WE WONT GO

I join in, feeling so full of pride I could burst. The first officer and his men start toward us as we chant, but when another police cruiser pulls up, they stop short. I even see a TV camera.

Mr. Miller looks confused, still holding firm to the hose.

"All I'm doing is protecting our rights," he tells the new policeman.

"You got no right to hose these people, Harry," he says to Mr. Miller. "Now put it away."

This officer orders the other cops to get back into their cruisers.

That's when I break the chain and run toward them.

"You need to check that hose, officer. It's got DDT in it."

"What?" a reporter standing by asks.

"Yes. I heard him and Mr. Anderson planning it last week. They put 50 percent DDT in that hose. You can check it for yourself."

"He's lying," Mr. Miller shouts.

"Move aside, Harry," says the officer. He calls over a few men to unscrew the hose.

"We'll get this tested at the lab," says the officer.

He takes Mr. Miller and Mr. Anderson into custody.

"What are you doing?" Mr. Miller snaps, trying to resist being handcuffed. "You have no evidence to arrest me."

That's when Teeter runs up with the shopping bag and pulls out the container he stole from Mr. Miller's shed.

"Here," he says, out of breath. "We found it in the shed behind the store."

The officer takes the container. "We'll test this. too. If it's the same stuff as in the hose—"

"You gonna believe some colored kid over me?" Mr. Miller complains.

"If you didn't plan to do something to these people, Harry, what're you doing out here?"

Mr. Miller doesn't respond.

"We'll figure it all out downtown," says the officer as he puts Mr. Miller and Mr. Anderson in the cruiser and then disperses the crowd.

I turn to Winston and shake his hand, like I want to pull it clean off.

"What made you come?"

He shrugs. "Boz got us to thinking. Just seemed like the right thing to do."

I pat him on the back, along with the rest of the guys. Billy and Hank are the only ones missing. Figures. They're losers, just like my sister says. When Bosley and I come face-to-face, we pause and then lock in a big bear hug.

"You're tops, Boz. Tops."

"I know I was dumb to stop being your friend—"

"Forget it. Coming here showed me what kind of friend you are."

"See you at practice?" he says.

"You bet you will."

I look around the crowd. I've got to find Eddie. Did he see the guys show up?

Then I spot him across the street. He's with Teeter, and they're coming toward me. We meet in the middle. Silence lingers between me and Eddie for a moment.

"Guess you're okay after all," he says to me.

I smile, and next thing you know, we grab each other's arms. Then I recall what Mr. Harrison said about trust: it comes from action, not words. Guess that's what Eddie needed to see.

"I could use your protesting skills," I tell him.

"For what?"

"Mr. Rogers says he's closing, and if you like those fried bologna sandwiches as much as I do, you'll help us fight to keep it open."

"You got it, my brother. We're a team on that one."

Eddie and I shake again and pat each other's shoulders, and then he and Teeter rejoin the marchers. I watch him go, glad that we're finally friends. All three of us.

I'm so happy I forget all about the fact that now I don't have a job. When it pops into my head, I sigh. I'll worry about that later. I don't want anything to spoil this day.

"Come on, son," says a man's voice behind me. It's Nick. "We've got to get to the hospital."

"Why? I'm not hurt." I glance down at my arms and legs to make sure I'm right.

"It's not about you, son. It's your mother."

I get in the back of Nick's cruiser, and we head to Jackson, the white hospital. When we get to the large glass doors, I hesitate.

"Don't worry, son. They'll let you see her," Nick reassures me.

The hospital is stark white and smells of Pine-Sol. My shoes slide on the slick, shiny floors as I hurry to get to Mama's room. I see her. She's lying in an all-white bed with tubes going everywhere. My stomach turns, and I get light-headed.

"Oh, Mama. Mama. It's Mark, Mama." I lean over the bed rail and whisper to her, but she doesn't respond to my voice.

"We're doing all we can, son." The doctor comes in behind me and puts his hand on my shoulder. "Don't give up hope."

I turn to him with questioning eyes.

"We've tried a new therapy, and we're confident that it's going to work. Don't worry. Don't worry..."

———

It's been twenty-four hours since I heard that doctor tell me not to worry. Now I sit in the apartment with Melissa. She turns on the black and white TV in front of us, but I'm not watching.

"...officials say the demonstrators might not have had a chance if not for the heroic actions of a local baseball team..."

"...firemen from Engine House 53 planned to launch powerful amounts of DDT-laced water into the crowd..."

"...one march organizer said he was appalled at the men, whom he called white supremacists."

"If not for those brave boys, there's no telling what might have happened. We'd like to say thank you to them for allowing us to have a peaceful march..."

Peaceful. That word penetrates my mind as we wait for somebody called a social worker to come.

Mama always said that if she ever died, the place she was going to would be peaceful.

Just then, the television signal goes out, leaving a screen full of snow. Millions of black and white dots all crammed together. My eyes fill with tears that blur my vision until all the dots merge together into one hazy blob of grey.

DISCUSSION

Now that you have read As Grey As Black and White, you may want to use the following discussion questions in class or during your book club meetings:

1. Why did Mark resist the fact that he was colored? What did he believe he had to lose?

2. How did Billy Justice come to have a racist attitude toward colored people, even his own team mates?

3. What factors led to the delay of school integration in Montgomery, Alabama?

4. What was Eddie Goshay really demonstrating against during the marches in front of local stores?

5. Why was Peter not interested in kowtowing to white people?

6. Could Mr. Miller be considered a 'typical' white southerner of that era? Why or why not?

7. What kind of teacher was Miss Alice May? Mr. Jordan? Mr. Harrison? How might their style of teaching differ from other schools?

8. Who was Johnnie Carr and how was she able to bring a lawsuit against the Montgomery County Board of Education?

9. What did Johnny Mack's attitude toward Mark indicate?

AFTERWORD

What's Happening in 1966?

In 1966, Americans are about to enter one of the most tumultuous times of the 20th century.

Thousands have already died in the Vietnam War and more than 6,000 lives will be lost this year alone. Activism is becoming a popular means of dissent and Americans take full advantage of it. Anti-War demonstrations gain momentum against the government's continuing belief that the war can be won. The Civil Rights movement continues in the South, the National Organization for Women is founded, and a 12-day transit workers strike shuts down the New York City subway.

But along with these acts of defiance comes opposition. James Meredith, the first student to integrate the University of Mississippi, is shot by a white supremacist during a march this year. Twelve southern school districts lose federal funding for violating the Civil Rights Act of 1964, and across the country, race riots begin, brought on by anger and impatience with the civil disobedience of Dr. King, leading to what becomes known as the 'long hot summer' of 1967.

This frustration and anxiety gives rise to alternative forms of resistance: the Nation of Islam, which espouses black separatism from 'white' Christianity, and The Black Power movement, headed by

Student Nonviolent Coordinating Committee (SNCC) leader, Stokely Carmichael, who coins the term 'black power' this year.

New fashions emerge, like the miniskirt and the Nehru jacket, influenced by London designers and the Mod scene taking root on the West Coast.

A growing counterculture is making inroads on college campuses encouraging young people to be wary of 'the establishment', not to 'trust anyone over 30' and to free their minds through drug experimentation. Additionally, prescription drug use and abuse is on the rise.

Musically, Janis Joplin performs her first concert. The Doors record their first album. And the Rolling Stones are growing in popularity. Beatle mania dies down, leading to their last US appearance this year. Contributing to their downfall is John Lennon's statement that the Beatles are "More popular than Jesus." This causes a backlash at southern radio stations which stop playing their records.

It's the year of significant government rulings beyond the civil rights of colored people. One such ruling is *Miranda v. Arizona* , which requires police to read an arrest victim their rights.

Escapist programming appears on TV and in theaters, such as *Star Trek, Lost in Space* and *Batman: The Movie.* Even the first soft landing on the moon takes place this year, giving the Soviets the upper hand in the space race.

Rural America also faces change as farms are subsidized by the government to plant fewer crops, and farm machinery reduces the need for sharecroppers and tenant farmers, forcing many to relocate to the cities for work.

And in sports, the Baltimore Orioles sweep the Los Angeles Dodgers in game four of the World Series, capturing their first championship in franchise history. Cassius Clay is stripped of his heavy weight boxing title after he refuses the draft. And the NFL joins the AFL, leading to the very first Super Bowl game the following month.

It all happens in 1966...

————

Freedom of Choice

Freedom of Choice is a desegregation plan used by the board of education after a federal judge rules in favor of, *Carr v. The Montgomery County Board of Education*. In this case, a colored woman sues on behalf of her son that the dual school system in the county violates Brown v. The Board of Education.

In the mid-60s, local school boards across the South use this tactic to maintain segregation. Under the plan, students over the age of 15, if not opposed by the parent, can choose where they want to attend school. It transfers the responsibility of integration to the student, and in most cases, it is hoped that each child will choose to attend a school with 'their own kind'.

In Montgomery, students can only choose their school during the month of April. After the 30th they can still make a choice but are added to a waiting list behind students who applied before the deadline.

The choice plan only applies to high school students since the board of education refuses to integrate the 5th or 6th grades until the 1967-68 school year.

The tactic works in Montgomery, Alabama. At the end of the first year, not one white student chooses to attend a colored school while a small percentage of colored children choose white schools.

The school board retains the right to deny a student's choice if they deem the desired school overcrowded. Some white schools are built small to achieve this goal. In '67, Jefferson Davis High is built to a size only large enough to house the white students within its white neighborhood. Yet, in 1968 it's forced to open as integrated.

Carr v. The Montgomery County Board of Education

In 1964, mother and Civil Rights activist, Johnnie Carr files a lawsuit on behalf of her son, Arlam, against the Montgomery County Board of Education. This case opens the way for school integration in the city. The courts finally rule in favor of Carr in 1966, forcing the school board to develop a plan for integration. Freedom of Choice is part of that desegregation plan.

Among the charges against the board are: the operation of a dual school system based on race and color; colored teachers are only assigned to colored schools; school buses are assigned according to race and those buses only transport colored children to colored schools; attendance areas are drawn to keep the races separate; and colored children who live near a white school are sent to a colored one further away.

Another charge by the Carr case is inadequate school facilities for colored children compared to white. As a result, twenty colored schools are slated to close; seven do so in the 1966-67 school year.

The Carr ruling is significant despite the fact that only 'token' integration takes place in those early years. Despite several court orders, between 1966 and 1968, data shows that Montgomery continues to operate a dual school system much like the one in place in 1964. It isn't until the mid-70s that Montgomery fully and completely complies with court rulings.

As part of this first ruling, Carr's son, Arlam Carr, Jr., is able to attend Sidney Lanier High School and becomes one of the first black students to graduate from the formerly all-white school. Some who also attend after the initial ruling, are so intimidated by racism, they leave before ever graduating.

White Flight and Segregated Academies
After the Carr ruling, white Montgomery parents change their rhetoric, moving from outright racism, to support of neighborhood schools. The idea being that it is safer for children to be close to home in case of emergencies. Yet, this concept is already in place for white students but is championed to avoid segregation — socioeconomics would dictate that most colored students will be forced to attend colored schools since only colored schools exist in their neighborhoods. But the courts circumvent this effort, by requiring students be bused in order to facilitate integration. In later years, after integration is moderately achieved, the court allows neighborhood elementary schools citing the reasonableness of having younger children attend school close to home.

Realizing that the courts were not going to ease up on the city school system, many white parents exercise the one alternative they have left: move outside the court's jurisdiction and enroll their children in what is known as 'segregated academies.'

These suburban, private schools provide white parents, who can afford to move, the solution to race mixing. Several Christian academies spring up in the mid- to late 60s to accommodate these parents. Montgomery Academy has been in existence as a private school for decades but receives state accreditation in 1965.

Things fall into place for whites seeking to leave the city. FHA regulations make it easier to afford a home. The interstate highway system encourages commuting, and an increased availability of automobiles means no need to ride public transportation with coloreds.

Between the 1950s and the 1970s, migration to outlying counties grows exponentially. This migration from the city to the suburbs, often known as 'white flight,' is the catalyst that alters the city's landscape and its white population in the years to come.

Public Discrimination in Parks and Recreation

One of the most visible sign of segregation, especially for Montgomery's school age children, is the closing of the public parks and other facilities.

Jim Crow laws enacted all over the South, have kept coloreds out of public libraries, buses and recreational facilities for decades. True, that before the 1964 ruling in *Brown v. The Board of Education*, some merchants, such as motels might allow coloreds to spend the night. But these facilities completely barred coloreds in retaliation for Brown.

In 1958, Montgomery city commissioners close all the public parks and even fill in the local swimming pool. Despite the 1896 ruling in *Plessy v. Ferguson* that required equal facilities for blacks, this rarely if ever happened. The city zoo, known as Oak Park Zoo, is also closed rather than admit coloreds. Steps are taken to sell off all the animals or transfer them to other zoos. All because of a ruling in a case brought by a colored hospital worker. He sued after he was arrested for simply walking through the park to get to work. No discussion of reopening these facilities takes place until lower and middle class white residents complain, since they cannot afford to join the city's private, segregated clubs frequented by Montgomery's upper class.

In 1965, some of these facilities are reopened to both white and colored; however, the zoo does not open until 1972. When it does, it is renamed Montgomery Children's Zoo.

Even after court mandates, school athletic programs continue to segregate. These sports activities are run by associations – one white and one colored. Under white association rules, white school teams are penalized if they play against teams of another race. Subsequently, white teams played only white teams, and colored teams played only colored.

Civil Disobedience and Black Power

For more than a decade, civil disobedience is the approach of most southern blacks, led by Dr. Martin Luther King, Jr. and other ministers. Its tenets include not resisting when arrested, not fighting back when beaten, and not using violence against your oppressors. The idea is that this type of activity will eventually cause white consciences to see reason, repent as it were, and stop mistreating their fellow black citizens. In effect, they'll be shamed.

But progress is coming too slow for many young blacks, including some who initially join King's movement. One such person is Stokely Carmichael, a young member of the Student Nonviolent Coordinating Committee. Carmichael and other students stage sit-ins to force whites to serve them at stores, restaurants and hospital waiting rooms slated as whites-only.

But when the students attempt registering blacks to vote, these efforts are not fully supported by the government, despite its initial promise to protect them. As a result, activists are beaten, hosed and humiliated. The aftermath of these events influences young black leaders to change their tactics, calling for self-pride and the need for a black political party. In 1966, Carmichael coins the term 'black power,' to express this need.

Across the country, black activists are getting tired of waiting on the slow progress of civil disobedience, the lack of support and protection from the US government, and older leaders continually telling them to wait, be patient, and go slow. From the late 60s onward, these leaders want equality, recognizing the need to accomplish this without the help of white liberals. This change in focus is leading to African pride — including embracing the Motherland by donning afros, braids and dashikis, and immersing themselves in the African arts. It also spawns black nationalism, and even a self-determination to get theirs 'by any means necessary.'

Walter White

Walter White was a mulatto who fought to end segregation prior to the 1960s. He was born in 1893 to slaves but raised to have pride in his colored heritage.

Historical records show that White was the great-grandson of William Henry Harrison, the ninth president of the United States.

He rose through the ranks to become the executive secretary for the National Association for the Advancement of Colored People (NAACP), a position he held from 1931 to 1955.

He first became affiliated with the Civil rights group in 1918 after graduating from Atlanta University.

White often gathered information against white supremacists by infiltrating their meetings and gatherings. It was all due to his ability to pass. His blonde hair, blue eyes and unquestionable resemblance to other southern whites, helped him to achieve his goal to investigate lynchers and bring them to justice.

In Montgomery, the record of lynchings is well-documented at The National Memorial for Peace and Justice. Located on the site of a former warehouse where blacks were enslaved, what is known as the national lynching memorial, houses 800 six-foot monuments symbolizing the thousands who died across the country.

Between 1877 and 1950, more than 4,000 African American men, women and children were hanged, burned alive, shot, drowned and beaten.

White's investigations of lynchings was particularly dangerous since he was often able to interview racist politicians and suspects accused in lynchings. On one occasion in 1919, he was discovered but was tipped off in advance so that he could escape the danger.

Among the events White influenced was the failed confirmation of Judge John Parker to the Supreme Court, the executive order by Franklin Roosevelt Fair Employment Practices Act of 1941, and he worked with such equality advocates as Eleanor Roosevelt.

White wrote a number of books about lynching and passing for white, as well as his own autobiography, *A Man Called White*.

Walter White died of a heart attack in 1955 at the age of 61.

Juliette Hampton Morgan

Unbeknownst to many who watch the attack of Civil Rights workers on national news or read about them in the newspapers, not all white Alabamans are against integration. In fact, one woman, Juliette Hampton Morgan, was a pioneer in the fight against discrimination as early as the 1940s.

Some well-to-do Montgomery residents, like Morgan, are not as quick to support segregation as their low and middle-class counterparts. Thus, Morgan takes a firm stand against the hatred she sees, by writing numerous letters to the local paper, *The Montgomery Advertiser*.

Mrs. Morgan was a 7th generation southerner and a 3rd generation Alabaman. She was college educated, a socialite, and associated with the rich and famous, including Zelda and F. Scott Fitzgerald.

But Morgan tells the paper that the injustices she witnesses daily on public transportation (she did not drive) moved her to speak out. She told of instances where a colored person paid the fare and when they stepped off to go to the back door of the bus, the driver would pull off.

At that time, coloreds are not allowed to enter the bus from the front nor ride in the areas designated for whites. During one such occasion, Morgan pulls the emergency cord, forcing the bus to stop and demanding the driver open the door for the colored woman he tries to abandon.

Morgan pays dearly for this and other actions, as opposition to her outspokenness grows. She loses her job and after humiliation and ridicule from groups like the White Citizen's Council, she takes her own life.

Morgan and many others white sympathizers of the Civil Rights movement suffer for the stand they take against oppression.

Dichlorodiphenyltrichloroethane (DDT)

In 1966, steps are already underway to limit the use of dichlorodiphenyltrichloroethane, better known as DDT.

This colorless, tasteless, odorless synthetic insecticide was used widely in the 1940s after it was used during World War II to treat body lice, bubonic plague, typhus and malaria.

It was also used as a pesticide on farms, and eventually made its way into homes as a household pest control product.

A 1966 international convention, led by the United Nations, seeks to limit the use of DDT but an exception is sought for its use in the treatment of malaria, since it has been highly effective in reducing the number of deaths from that illness.

DDT works by affecting the nervous system of insects, interfering with normal nerve processes. Insects exposed to DDT have tremors, convulsions and hyper excitability. Extended exposure is found to cause liver lesions and tumors in animals.

The human effects are not as evident, especially in the short term, but scientists such as Rachel Carson sought to turn the public's attention to its long term effects. In her book, *Silent Spring*, Carson paints a grim picture of how prolonged exposure to DDT would cause any number of crippling results to humans. What is known is that these effects are not life threatening and can cause exposed individuals to experience side effects like headaches, nausea, vomiting, to name just a few.

But Carson's book coupled with a CBS report which aired in September 1963, creates a public outcry calling for a ban of the pesticide.

In large doses, DDT can be fatal. The lethal dose, LD50, is 50% toxicity. In the 1960s no evidence is found linking short or long term levels of DDT to human fatality.

Another concern is that DDT remains in the environment for many years. It wasn't until 1972 that the US government admitted the pesticide's long term effects on humans or the environment.

ACKNOWLEDGMENTS

At this time, I would like to thank the following people for their help, support and advice over the past five years as I hammered out this manuscript:

- Atlanta Writer's Club
- Liz Parker, Author Mentor Match mentor
- The Cincinnati chapter of SCBWI
- Shanna Hughes, #DVPit
- Jenny Bowman, Carol Taylor and every other editor I've forgotten

ABOUT THE AUTHOR

Faith Knight writes YA and Adult fiction. She lives in North Carolina with her husband. Get her other books, learn of new projects, and sign up for her newsletter at http://www.therealknightauthor.com